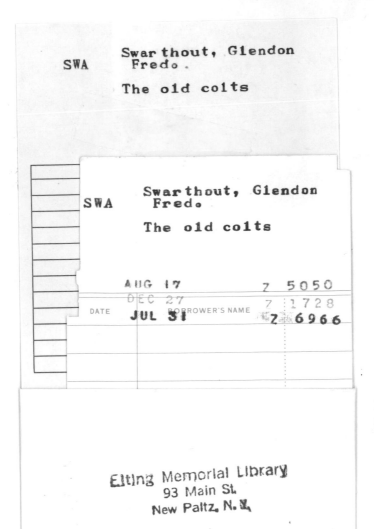

SWA   Swarthout, Glendon
       Fredo.

       The old colts

SWA   Swarthout, Glendon
       Fredo.

       The old colts

AUG 17   7 5050
DEC 27   7 1728
DATE JUL 31 BORROWER'S NAME 7 6966

© THE BAKER & TAYLOR CO.

THE OLD COLTS

By Glendon Swarthout

WILLOW RUN
THEY CAME TO CORDURA
WHERE THE BOYS ARE
WELCOME TO THEBES
THE CADILLAC COWBOYS
THE EAGLE AND THE IRON CROSS
LOVELAND
BLESS THE BEASTS AND CHILDREN
THE TIN LIZZIE TROOP
LUCK AND PLUCK
THE SHOOTIST
THE MELODEON
SKELETON
THE OLD COLTS

THE OLD COLTS

☆

Glendon Swarthout

DONALD I. FINE, INC.
New York

for
Michael Zimring

The Knight's Tale

*May, with alle thy floures and thy
    grene,
Welcome be thou, faire, fresshe May.*

Author's Note

I met Walter Winchell one fine afternoon in October of
1970. I was introduced to him by a barber while having
my hair styled at the O.K. Tonsorial Corral in Scottsdale,
Arizona.

We chatted. That I was a novelist interested him in
general, that my subjects had sometimes been shoot-'em-
up in particular. His shave and manicure completed,
Winchell donned a snap-brim hat of black straw, waited,
and when my barber concluded his ministrations, invited
me to his home for a drink—a chance at which I jumped.
(I had lived in Scottsdale eleven years. The ex-big-name-
columnist-broadcaster had long maintained a residence in
"The West's Most Western Town" for his wife, whose
respiratory problems were alleviated by the arid climate,
and he lived alone there now, in retirement.)

I followed him in my car to his home. We had a drink.
(He wore a shroud-colored cashmere jacket with black
pocket square, white shirt, black four-in-hand, black
shantung slacks, slip-on shoes of black alligator, and did
not remove his black hat—the rig was as funereal as the
atmosphere of the house.) At seventy-two, Winchell was
but the casing of the bullet he once had been. His wife
had passed away the preceding year. His son had sui-
cided the Christmas before that. His relationship with
his daughter was cat-and-dog. Cancer, and a broken heart,

7

would kill him soon, in February of 1972, and there would be only two mourners at his burial site in Greenwood Memorial Park, Phoenix.

"You ever heard of an old Western character named Bat Masterson?" he asked, his voice scratchy.

"I surely have."

(I had indeed. The life of William Barclay "Bat" Masterson was about as I'll-be-damned as any ever lived by an American. He was sheriff and marshal in wild and woolly Kansas, ranked with Wyatt Earp among the most mythical lawmen of their lawless day. But he was also buffalo hunter, Indian fighter, army scout, gambler, shootist, and prizefight promoter in the West before absquatulating in his middle years to—of all places, with a derby hat on his head and the six-gun at his hip which promptly got him thrown in the jug—New York City. Here, too, his career was a jaw-dropper. In a gilded age of journalism he won his own celebrity as sports columnist for the *Morning Telegraph*. He became a friend of the famous, as welcome at the Waldorf-Astoria and the White House as he earlier had been at the Long Branch Saloon in Dodge City. For two decades he glowed as incandescently as the Edison bulbs along the "Gay White Way.")

"I'm a Bat buff, in fact," I went on to Winchell. "Read everything in print about Earp and Masterson and the Dodge City days. I know the Lake and O'Connor biographies by heart." (Lake, Stuart N., *Wyatt Earp: Frontier Marshal*, Boston, 1931; O'Connor, Richard, *Bat Masterson*, New York, 1957.) I was curious of course. "Why do you ask?"

"I've got something of his," was the response. "Kind of a true story he wrote down in his last years."

"Masterson? In his own hand?"

"You heard me. And I have to trust it to somebody—

8

I'm not long for this world." At my demur he pushed up his hat. "I should know, shouldn't I?" This came with a bit of his old belligerence. "Here." He bent, took a manila folder from a cabinet beside him, and stood with it in his hand. "Would you like to own it?"

"Would I!"

"Will you swear never to publish it?"

I hesitated.

"Shit or say yes, Swarthout."

"Yes."

"Okay, you got it."

I laid the folder in my lap. If I was dizzy, it was not the drink. That I was in the company of Walter Winchell was improbable. That he should make me a gift of holograph pages purportedly composed by Bat Masterson was impossible. I sparred for time and a clear head. "How did you come by this?"

He sat down again. "Damon Runyon. One night— 1945 I think it was—Damon and I were in the Cub Room at the Stork. Sherm Billingsley had left our table to make the rounds and we were alone. Runyon couldn't talk then—he was dying of throat cancer—had to write everything out on a pad. So he gave me the four pages in that folder and wrote out whose they were and how he got 'em and asked me not to print 'em after he was gone."

"Why you?"

"Because I was his best pal. He was divorced, he had nobody to leave anything to. He was in the same sad shape I am now."

"Why not a library?"

"You'll see when you read—it's kind of a true confession by the old boy. The Western history big shots see it and they'd blow their stacks. Also because Masterson and I both used to work for the same paper, the *Telegraph*, believe it or not. He was before my time, but later, in the late Twenties, I was trying to get out of my contract with the *Graphic*—they were paying me peanuts—and Gene Fowler, editor of the *Telegraph* then, let me write an unsigned column so I could make some more dough. I called it 'Beau Broadway.' Anyway, Masterson and I both worked for the same rag, at different times. Colleagues, you might say. So Runyon knew I'd take good care of this thing."

I had to ask. "He took your word you wouldn't print, ever?"

His eyes flashed with their former fire. "If I told Damon I wouldn't, I goddamn wouldn't."

I nodded an apology.

"Well, you gonna read or not?" he challenged.

"One more question, Mr. Winchell. How did Damon Runyon get these pages?"

"What's it to you?"

"How do we know they're not a forgery?"

He glared at me. "Runyon bought 'em in 1931. For a thousand bucks. From Emma Masterson, the widow."

"Mrs. Masterson herself?"

"Runyon never lied to me in his life."

"I see." (It was plausible. I had read that one reason Runyon and Masterson, despite the age difference, became fast friends in New York was because both were western in origin. Bat, the plainsman, reminded Runyon of his father, a frontier editor whom he idolized. Al Runyon had been born and raised in Colorado, and did not take the name Damon till he gravitated east from Denver in 1911. Bat was a boy in Kansas, and during his gunpowder period gambled and kept the peace in such Colorado mining camps as Creede and Trinidad in addition to boomtown Denver. Such bosom buddies were they that on Bat's death on October 25, 1921—suddenly, at sixty-eight, of a heart attack, at his pigeonhole desk in the *Telegraph* offices—Runyon sat up all night beside the casket while hundreds of the high and low filed through Campbell's Funeral Parlor. It was logical Mrs. Masterson would go to the newsman with a legacy of this sort. And the year 1931 satisfied the chronology. I knew Bat and his missus had occupied an apartment at 300 West 49th Street until the old gunfighter kicked the bucket, and that Emma Masterson lived out a pinched and lonely widowhood until her own demise in 1932.)

"Well?" demanded Winchell.

"I'm ready," I replied. I genuflected to the gods, girded my intellectual loins, and took up the folder.

To this day I wish to God I had not. To this day I wish I had spurned the gift. I did not have then, nor have I now, any desire to cut a notch in anyone's reputation. I delight in the "Bat" of legend. I should be honored to meet the Masterson of fact. But what I now owned, and what I was about to read, was a document so shocking that it spun the mind like the cylinder of a revolver. It smashed to smithereens. It turned Mr. Masterson, at least temporarily, into a total stranger. Should it be the real thing, I realized at once, it had surpassing historical significance. In order to possess the document, however, I had just promised Winchell never to publish it. I had therefore sentenced myself to sit in agony for the next fourteen years astride the longhorns of a dilemma. If I kept my word to him, would I not throttle a truth which should be told? Rob the bank of American history? If I broke it, on the other hand, if I succumbed to the scholar's temptation and let the cat out of the bag, would that not make the memory of a remarkable American character into a cuspidor? Desecrate a hero's grave?

(To some of us, I am ashamed to say, ink is more potent than blood, and publication a lure more irresistible than lust. In the end I would succumb.)

I opened the folder. There were four pages of lined foolscap, torn evidently from a copy pad of the sort available in any newsroom. The paper was yellow, the ink a faded brown, the script neat and entirely legible. I looked first at the fourth page. It was signed at the bottom "W.B. Masterson," his habitual signature, which anyone might have duplicated, and was dated "May 7, 1916," which signified nothing. But the first page was headed "300 W. 49th St."

The palms of my hands damped. I closed my eyes, opened them, tried to quell my pulse and put a lid on my blood pressure, then began to read.

Halfway down the first page I encountered a name which took my breath away. I looked up at the waiting Walter Winchell.

"My God!" I gasped.

"I told you so!" he scratched.

When I had finished the four pages I looked up again, around the room, out the windows at the milky distant mountains, as though to establish my own time and place and credibility.

"I'll be damned," I said.

I thanked Winchell profusely that day in 1970, promised a second time never to go to press with the Masterson manuscript, took my leave and the precious pages home in palsied hands.

I was in a fever to authenticate them. That very evening

I masked all but ten lines of page one, photocopied them, and sent them with an urgent request to Joseph W. Snell, Executive Director of the Kansas State Historical Society in Topeka, a friend and the country's ultimate authority on the Mastersons, Bat and his brothers Ed and Jim. Would he please have these ten lines checked against whatever he could find in Bat's hand immediately if not sooner?

His response was weeks in coming, but he is a scholar and a gentleman and my heart leap'd up when I beheld his verdict: Yes, irrefutably, based on both internal evidence (personal and topical references only Bat could have made) and on the science of calligraphy, this was William Barclay Masterson on paper. Not only had the Society's handwriting expert compared it with the signatures and lines extant on writs and pay vouchers surviving in the official records of Ford County, Kansas (which Bat served as sheriff in the late 1870's), but he had sent it on to the Connecticut State Library, where is preserved the 1885 letter by Bat to the Colt company ordering a special pistol "easy on Trigger," and calligraphists there, after close comparison, declared my ten lines good as gold.

Joe Snell was understandably excited, and buckshot me with questions. What had I stumbled on? Where? How? What was its length? Was there a book in it? When would I publish? I must know that such a find was a priceless piece of Americana. I must recognize that rumors of the discovery would create a ruckus in the Western historical community.

I sent him sad news. My lips were sealed.

But like murder, rumor will out, and in the next year or two I had hot letters of inquiry from curators, archivists, librarians, collectors, dealers, paperback amateurs, and leather-bound professionals. I made no reply whatever. I let them stew in their own jealous juices. I kept my word to Walter Winchell, hence his to Damon Runyon, and Runyon's, probably, to Emma Masterson. I locked the four pages in my safe, where they ticked away like a detonative device.

300 WEST 49th STREET

☆

"Mr. Masterson?"

Bat cocks an eye.

"Guy to see you."

"Collector?"

"You can smell 'em a mile away—so I set him up." The copy boy is sixteen and Lower East Side and his name is Sammy Taub. "Told him you'd never sell it—not for love or lucre."

"Attaboy."

"Say, Mr. Masterson, would you put in a good word for me with Mr. Lewis? I don't wanna be a copy boy all my life."

"What do you want?"

"A beat. City Hall, PD, maybe sports, like you."

"Okeh. You get a little fur on your upper lip and we'll see. Now send the gink in."

"Yessir. Same split?"

"You got it."

Sammy's head snaps from the doorway as though by rubber band and Bat opens a deep drawer in his pigeon-hole desk. It contains an arsenal of old Colt revolvers. Taking the one on top, closing the drawer, checking the grip for notches, he lays the Peacemaker on the desk in museum view and resumes, with Parker pen on yellow copy pad, his journalistic labors.

"Mr. Masterson?"

Bat cocks an eye.

"Bat Masterson?"

16

They came to the offices of the *Telegraph*, **once a carbarn** at West 50th and Eighth Avenue, every week or so the year round, and for the same reason. This was a dressy, flashy, wheezy gent down from Waltham, Mass., who played with a pearl stickpin and popped sweat the second he had a gander at the weapon on the desk. A seat was proffered. He settled into it. Said it was an honor and a privilege to meet Bat Masterson. Said he was a student of the West, regretful he had never had an opportunity to partake of its adventure and romance. Said he would like to "palaver" a little about the old days. Bat said shoot. They talked about Dodge and Wyatt Earp and the killing of Sergeant King in Sweetwater, Texas, when Molly Brennan gave her life for Bat's, and the scrap at Adobe Walls where Bat and a handful of buffalo hunters held off a horde of redskins and the rescue of the Germain sisters from the Cheyenne while Bat was a scout for General Miles.

"Earp was your friend."

"My best."

"He's the other one I'd like to meet. Saw somewhere he lives in California."

"I heard he does."

The gent glanced at the gun on the desk, glanced away. "Don't you miss those times, Mr. Masterson?"

"Not a damn. I'm a New Yorker now."

"How long have you lived here?"

"Fourteen years."

"I declare, I don't know how a rough customer like you—begging your pardon—a man with a past like yours

17

winds up on a newspaper in New York."

"Luck and talent."

"Pretty tame though, ain't it? I mean, compared to the wide open spaces?"

"I hope I never see those dreary old prairies again."

"Er, uh, is that your gun?"

"It is."

"Mind if I have a look?"

Bat passed it over.

The hands trembled. The cylinder was turned, the weapon hefted. A fat index finger worked its way down the grip, counting the notches.

"Twenty-three," Bat supplied.

A wheeze, of pleasure and confirmation. "You killed twenty-three men!"

Bat shrugged.

"I must tell you, sir, I collect a few guns. On an amateur basis, of course. Mr. Masterson, I will give you fifty dollars for this gun."

"Not that one, you won't."

"But I can buy one like it—identical—in any pawnshop for ten."

"Not that one, you can't."

"Why not?"

Bat set the hook. "That was the gun killed Walker and Wagner after they killed my brother Ed."

"Is that a fact?" The listener was all ears, including lobes. He knew the story by rote, but hungered for it first-hand.

Bat reeled the line in slowly but succinctly: how Ed Masterson, serving as deputy marshal, had been sur-rounded by six Texans outside the Lady Gay in Dodge one drunken night in '78 and gutshot by Walker or Wagner at such close range that his coat was set ablaze; how Bat came on the run and fired four rounds from sixty feet in semi-darkness; how one shot felled Wagner, who died the next day, and three Walker, who lingered a month with a hole in his lung before expiring; and how—here the narrator lowered the brim of his hat to half-mast and let his voice break ever so slightly—Ed passed on within half an hour, in the arms of his younger brother, who wept like a child. By this grand finale the gun collector had out a silk handkerchief and was bailing both cheeks.

"Mr. Masterson," said he, "I will give you a hundred dollars for this gun."

Derby down, Bat sat for a spell as though whipsawed by emotion and economics. "I am a little low on funds at the moment," he muttered at length. "Let's see the color of your money."

"Gladly."

Sir Waltham of Mass. extricated ass from chair and wallet from hip. Licking a thumb, he laid two fifties on the desk like aces back-to-back.

"Mr. Masterson, I can't say—"

"Good day."

"I assure you, I will never part with this historic weapon. It will be handed down—"

"Get the hell on your horse."

"Yes, sir!"

Exit the gink.

Enter Sammy Taub. He was given a fiver, his usual cut of the take. He tucked it away, sucked a jujube, and contemplated his future.

"You won't forget about Mr. Lewis, sir?"

"Not me."

"How many guns you got left?"

"As many as you've got suckers."

Exit the boy, grinning, while Bat attended to the completion of his column. It ran daily, required two hours to write on average, and was called "Masterson's Views on Timely Topics"—which topics were invariably pugilistic. Bat had promoted fights and refereed fights and seconded fighters. He knew everyone in the game, from Jess Willard, the then heavyweight champ, to Tex Rickard, to the blind and pitiful pug who sold pencils outside Grupp's Gym on 116th St. When he pulled his editorial pistol he meant to use it, and did, to the woe of fakers and fixers and the glee of readers, so that his column was scripture in the city and widely quoted on the sports pages of other papers nationally. His subject this afternoon was the Sailor White vs. Victor McLaglen—billed as "The Actor-Heavyweight"— fracas upcoming at the Garden. He finished, scrawled a "30," pushed from the desk, left his office, strolled through the rivet of telephones and clack of typewriters and roar of reportorial brains that was the newsroom, dropped the pages into a wire basket on the city desk, reversed himself and would have departed for the day had he not been waved into a glassed-in office by the arm of W.E. Lewis, editor of the *Morning Telegraph*.

"You hooked another one."

"Why not?"

"How much?"

"A hundred."

20

"Bat, you have a larcenous heart."

"Look, he'll sell it tomorrow for two hundred."

W.E. tilted his chair. "I thought I should tell you. Reception called me a few minutes ago. Some guy was asking if Bat Masterson really works here. She said you do and did he want an appointment? But he just walked out on her. Odd."

"What'd he look like?"

"An outlander. Tall, she said. Lean. Your age, maybe a little older. She used the word 'grim'—said she wouldn't care to meet him in a dark alley."

They were old friends, Bat and W.E. Lewis. They had met in Dodge way back when. Lewis, then a newsman in Kansas City, had been prospecting the West for "color" for articles and wanted Bat to introduce him to the James brothers, who had just raided Northfield, Minnesota and ridden away with bloody noses and empty saddlebags. "I better not," Bat told him. "They'll be meaner than ever now. They'd eat you alive." It was good advice. Later, as editor and columnist, each was in the other's debt. It was Lewis who helped spring Bat from jail on his arrival in New York in 1902, and eventually gave him a crack at covering the fight game. In return, Bat lent Lewis's sheet, besides the renown of his name, an honesty and a dignity in exceeding short supply.

W.E. locked hands behind his head and studied the other over the rims of his specs. "Something's been eating you lately. Money? You can have an advance of salary anytime."

"I'm having a bum streak. I'll get lucky again. You know—feathers today, chicken tomorrow."

"That's what they all say."

"Listen," said Bat. "Once out in Dodge I had a badger in a barrel on Front Street and I put up a sign. I bet anybody with a dog their dog couldn't get my badger out of the barrel. Somebody'd come along nearly every day and put up ten bucks and drop their dog in the barrel. Well, they'd go at it, tooth and claw, and tip over the barrel and my animal would take off with the dog after him and I won't say how much I lost. But I had faith and finally got lucky."

"How?"

Bat grinned, tipped his hat, turned to go, and said, over his shoulder, "Shot the damn badger."

That evening he sashays into a small cigar store on 43rd Street, passes the counter and wooden Indian, and pushes through a swinging door into the back room, which is a race room.

On the walls are big boards for the tracks, with today's results and tomorrow's entries in chalk, and behind three desks are three bookies with eyeshades taking bets by telephone. At the rear of the room, wearing leather caps and playing three-cushion on a billiard table, are two muscular mugs who work for Grogan, and standing around considering the boards and talking about the liner *Cymric* being torpedoed off the Irish coast and figuring the forms are many strong men and weak, sure things in the stretch of life and longshots, men of character and men who'll bust a piggybank to get a bet down on a nag, any nag. The race room reeks of sweat, smoke, spit, and concentration, but to Bat the smells are bugles. Being here is the next best thing to being in a box at Belmont. He shoulders through to find the Pimlico board and scowls at what he finds in the fifth.

"Hiya, Mr. Masterson," says somebody.

"Masterson? Bat Masterson?" says somebody else, grabbing a bet slip and a pencil stub. "Gimme your autograph, Mr. Masterson?"

Bat obliges, then moves in on a desk as Eddie the Cuff hangs up the phone.

"You seen the Pimlico?" asks Eddie. "Cat's Pajamas was out front by four lengths—past the five-eighth pole broke a leg—had to shoot 'im—you had fifty."

"On the cuff, Eddie," says Bat.

Eddie shakes his head. "I can't—you said you'd cough up and you ain't, and Grogan says cash on the drum."

"On the cuff," says Bat. "And put fifty on Auntie Tan in the first tomorrow at 'Gansett."

Eddie shakes his head. "I can't, Bat—Grogan'd bust our balls, yours and mine both—he says you're into him too deep—your credit's no good anywheres."

Men are listening.

"Do it," says Bat.

"No," says Eddie.

Bat reaches, takes Eddie's neck in one hand, lifts him from his chair, and pulls his eyeshade down over his face with the other.

Men are watching.

"Place the bet," says Bat.

"Erahh, erahh," chokes Eddie.

The room hushes like a church. The two mugs who work for Knuckles Grogan stop playing three-cushion.

"Take it easy, old-timer," says one to Bat.

Men sidle silently out of the way and crouch behind desks and glue their butts to the walls.

Hands around the bookie's neck, Bat stares at the mugs. Pool cues at the ready, they stare at him. Something happens to Bat's eyes.

"Two things betokened the real man: his eyes," Irvin S.

23

Cobb will write of Bat in later life. "They were like smoothed ovals of gray schist with flecks of mica suddenly glittering in them if he were roused."

Bat's gray eyes glitter now.

"No, you take it easy," someone warns the mugs. "That's Bat Masterson."

A moment more. Then the mugs get smart and go back to three-cushion, and men move from the walls, and Bat loosens his grip.

"Okeh, okeh, Bat," hoarses Eddie the Cuff.

He is let go. He bumps his rump down, drags up his eyeshade, adjusts his sleeve-garters, and swallows a frog of fright.

Bat outs with a roll of singles and two fresh fifties and peels the fifties onto the bookie's desk.

"Now we got that straight," says the ex-marshal, "here's Cat's Pajamas today and Auntie Tan tomorrow. In the first at 'Gansett. You tell Grogan I'll pay up when I'm damn good and ready. And tell him remember one thing. My name is my credit."

Heading east on 43rd Street his heart bangs and his legs are like an accordion because he's getting to be a little long in the tooth for such chip-on-the-shoulder stuff. It's an April night. The air is soft and sooty. Up front he can hear Times Square booming away like the Battle of Gettysburg and the spark and rumble of a trolley car somewhere behind. Suddenly the back of his neck tells him to stop, to turn. He stops, turns. Thirty paces to his rear a man has emerged from a doorway. By the light of a streetlamp they give each other a once-over, and a twice. Bat sees an individual in late middle age, tall and slab-sided, wearing a slouch hat, mismatched jacket and trousers, and a gray mustache thick enough to curry a horse. He recalls at once what Lewis said the receptionist said. An outlander. The word "grim." And wouldn't want to meet him in a dark alley. This is the guy all right. The guy, whoever he may be, sees a Masterson in late middle age, somewhat sawed-off and inclined to be stout, wearing a derby on the tilt, a natty cheviot suit, and a gray mustache clipped sharp enough to cut carrots. Having seen, the man turns, valise in hand, and eats up the street with his stride, heading west.

The rhythms of Bat Masterson's life in New York were not dissimilar to those of his Dodge City life in the salad-and-sulphur days. There he slept late in the morning, did the paperwork attendant on his duties as a lawman in town and county, saw to the prisoners in his hoosegow, presented himself officially at trials, and took care of personal business such as playing practical jokes, betting on a badger, and daily draw-and-accuracy practice. On occasion, alone or with a small posse, he took to the saddle in pursuit of train robbers such as Dave Rudabaugh, rustlers like the Lyons brothers, and murderers such as James Kennedy, who made the innocent mistake of killing Dora Hand, a "soiled dove," when he intended instead to eliminate Dog Kelley. Here, in the city, he slept late in the morning, strolled to the *Telegraph*, ground out his column, received visitors and sold guns, then went to gyms to watch fighters train, or regaled himself at the Belmont races during the season. On occasion he would handle a special assignment for Lewis, such as covering the trial for murder of Chester Gillette upstate—on which case and execution Theodore Dreiser later based his novel *An American Tragedy.*

His nights were a horse of another hue.

In Dodge, he made the rounds of saloons north of the "deadline," the Santa Fe tracks—the Alamo, Long Branch, Occident, Hoover's, Peacock's, Stock Exchange, St. James, to name seven of seventeen—and the dance houses and halls south, among them the Lady Gay, the Varieties, the Comique, and the Opera House. He sat in on a hand of cards or a case of faro. He disarmed drunks. He bonked obstreperous cowboys over the head with the barrel of a Colt and dragged them off to sweet dreams behind bars. When hot blood was being or about to be shed, he came on the run, gun drawn, and did, his cold crotch be damned, whatever dangerous he had to do. Sometimes the shout of "Here comes Masterson!" was sufficient to stay the triggers and lay the dust. Sometimes, unfortunately, it was not.

This was all very well for a young man full of piss and vinegar. To a man with a gray roof, nights in the Big Burg were more agreeable. He covered the important fights at the Stadium Athletic Club, at the National Sporting Club, at Madison Square Garden. He went often to the theater. Dramas were too "down-and-out" to his taste, but he doted on musicals like the Ziegfeld Follies, starring Fanny Brice and W.C. Fields, and C.B. Dillingham's extravaganzas at the Hippodrome, particularly "Hip-Hip-Hooray!" with its army of chorus girls parading to John Philip Sousa's band. He most pleasured himself, however, during the hours between the fights and the shows and the coming of the dawn. He made the rounds of the bars and cabarets and clubs and restaurants of the "Roaring Forties," that carnival of din and dazzle, that outrageous reach of Broadway between Madison and Times Squares, taking to the bright lights like a duck to water. He hobnobbed with magnates, jockeys, fight managers, financiers, agents, journalists, hookers, theatrical names, card sharks, chorines, detectives, tenors, playwrights, and bunco artists in Rector's, Shanley's, the Cafe des Beaux Arts, Delmonico's, the bars of the Hoffman House, the Waldorf, the Knickerbocker, the Astor, and a dozen more. He ran into friends. He drank, and appeared to have the capacity of a camel. He talked shop and swapped scoops. He concocted practical jokes, some of which went over big and some of which fell flat as a tire. He played poker, pulling plenty of pots at times, tapping out at others. He ate a breakfast of scrambled eggs and Irish bacon and steaming coffee at Jack Dunstan's in the wee hours and went home to bed with the milkwagons. "It's a great life if you don't weaken!" everyone who was anyone said in the New York of 1916, and Bat Masterson was determined to hang on to the merry-go-round six nights a week the year through till he fell off and the music stopped. He wasn't after the brass ring. He just loved the ride.

From cowtown to city, then, from Front Street to the "Gay White Way" was for Bat a hop-skip-and-jump. The Kansas farm boy turned out to be a born New Yorker. Out there he had worn a star. Here he had star billing from the day he hit Grand Central. Out there he bullied money from a cheapskate town council. Here it came easy, from the point of a pen. Out there the price of a high old time was too often paid in death rattles, while here dollar bills did the trick. Out there, in the end, a man might be planted in a pine box on Boot Hill. Here he got a satin-lined casket and interment in green and elegant Woodlawn. And one thing for sure, along the way here he kept a hell of a lot classier company.

27

His company in carouse was in the main that of other newsmen. There would have been a natural affinity in any case. Bat was a man's man, generous, outgoing, full of fun. He was the real thing, too. Soon after his arrival in Gotham the magazine *Human Life* signed him to do a series of articles on the celebrated gunmen he had known, from Clay Allison to Luke Short, from Ben Thompson to Wyatt Earp, and, when the pieces ran, even the most cynical reporter recognized the ring of truth in every line. When he went to work for the *Telegraph*, he wrote an honest column. And so his fellows welcomed him to their charmed and bibulous circle with a grin and a clap on the back and bought him a drink.

And he made marvelous copy. They knew he had actually slain only three men—Sergeant King and the assassins of his brother Ed—but it was they who pumped up the count to twenty-three on grounds that gore was a damn-sight more interesting to the reader than verisimilitude. It was they who expanded the Plunkett shootout into a front-page item. Some blowhard Coloradan by that moniker and a Texan named Dinklesheets were standing around at the Waldorf bar getting spifflicated and proclaiming that Bat Masterson was a fake and a fraud and his reputation in the West was lower than a snake's hips. After several nights of this, Bat confronted the pair with a hand thrust into his pocket. "Look out!" someone yelled, "Bat's going to flash his cannon!" There was a stampede for the exits, led by Plunkett and Dinklesheets, and when the shooting was over—there had been none whatever—and Bat was begged to put his cannon on public display, he smiled and pulled from his pocket a pack of Spuds.

Another reason why he was much cherished by his peers was that, since he was a newsman now, and you were a newsman, a little of his luster rubbed off on you. But for accident of birth, you might have had the adventures, you might be hustled by autograph hounds, you might be a Bat Masterson—and sometimes wished you were. Not least of all, you might be able to tell the tall tales he could. His yarns enraptured. Liarly though most might sound, they were based on experience no city slicker had ever had, and hence could not disprove.

To send cold chills up and down their spines he had only to describe in detail, for example, the killing of Levi Richardson by Frank Loving.

To make them slap their knees, he might recollect how they put a monkey in the room at the Dodge House of a drunkard drummer who had passed out, and what happened when he revived.

To split their sides, he could recall the amazing Prof. Geezler, the armless showman who wrote letters and rolled cigarettes and fired off a small howitzer with his toes, and prospered mightily until the night he had one too many before a performance in Wichita and blew off his act.

Bat could also pull his listeners' legs right out of their sockets.

Four ayem. He was in Jack Dunstan's, near the Hipp on Sixth Avenue, having breakfasted with Irvin S. Cobb, star rewrite man of the *World;* Hype Igoe, sportswriter on the same sheet, who liked to bring his ukelele to Jack's and lead the waiters in song; Wilson Mizner, playwright and short storyist who would become, in time, screenwriter and resident wit in Hollywood; Val O'Farrell, private eye and "friend" of Peggy Hopkins Joyce; Jimmy Walker, attorney and New York State Senator who even then aspired to be mayor one day; Damon Runyon of the *American;* and George M. Cohan, whose Revue had just passed a hundred performances at the Astor. They were watching a flying wedge of waiters bounce some disorderly college boys into Sixth Avenue and talking about the Sailor White vs. Victor McLaglen fight, and when Bat was asked what he would say about it in his column tomorrow, he said he had advised McLaglen to forget fighting and stick to the stage.

Just then he saw a tall man enter the place, the man in the slouch hat he had earlier encountered on 43rd Street outside the race room. Carrying the valise, the man approached the bar, pointed Bat out to a bartender, then was gone before Bat could get to the bar.

"That tall guy," Bat said to the bartender. "What'd he want?"

"Asked me if that was you. I said it was."

"Know 'im?"

"Not him."

When he returned to the table the others were drinking coffee and chewing the fat of two subjects simultaneously: the Peck murder case in Grand Rapids, Michigan, and Wilson's dawdling and inconsistent responses to Germany's submarine warfare on neutral shipping. After a tortuous trial a doctor named Waite had that day been found guilty of poisoning the Pecks, his wife's millionaire parents—a verdict O'Farrell had predicted—and that day, despite the torpedoing of the *Cymric,* the President had declared in a National Press Club speech that the U.S. should stay out of war in order to help Europe reinstate peace. The consensus at the table at that weary hour was that no one would ever really know whether or not Waite was guilty because the evidence was too complicated, and only events would tell whether or not Wilson was playing with all his marbles because the matter of neutral shipping in wartime was too complicated.

"Damn near as complicated as poling hogs," opined the *Telegraph* columnist.

There was a loud pause. The other seven at the table looked into their cups and settled their butts in preparation for another masterpiece of Mastersonia.

"What in hell is poling hogs?" asked Runyon, agreeable to being straight man.

Bat lit a Spud. "Well, in the northwest corner of Arkansas—"

"Hold it," said Igoe. "Just where is the northwest corner of Arkansas?"

"Well," said Bat, "suppose you're in the northwest corner of Oklahoma. To get to the northwest corner of Arkansas you go east till you smell it, then south till you step in it."

Hype nodded.

"I'll begin again," said Bat. "In the northwest corner of Arkansas there's a lot of acorn trees, and usually the boys in a family aren't weaned until they are eighteen or twenty years old."

They reflected.

"I don't get it," admitted O'Farrell, the ace detective.

Jimmy Walker, attorney and state senator, drew on a stogie. "Now just a minute." He addressed Bat like a witness. "Let's separate these things, shall we? Why are the boys in northwest Arkansas not weaned until they are eighteen or twenty years old?"

"Because the longer they're on mother's milk, the taller they grow, and the taller they grow, the more money they can earn."

They looked at each other, sinking ever deeper into the swamp, willing yet reluctant.

"Goddammit, Georgie," said Runyon to Cohan, "I will

31

not play straight man all the damn time. It's your turn."

George M. jumped out of his chair and leaned on its back. He was not a man who liked to sit when there was something going on, and something was. "All right, Bat," he said on cue. "I have never played northwest Arkansas and never intend to, but how can the boys there earn more money the taller they grow?"

"By poling hogs."

Bat smiled round the table as though that explained everything.

Hype Igoe strummed a discordant chord on his ukulele. "Oh my God," he groaned, "here we go again."

Bat took up the slack. "And the reason they can earn a lot of money poling hogs is because of the nature of the mud in Arkansas. It balls up easy, and hardens up like a brick."

"The mud! What in hell does mud have to do with—" Damon Runyon checked himself and glared through his glasses.

"Gentlemen, gentlemen," Cobb reproved in his grits-and-hominy drawl. "It is no use asking questions or exercising ourselves. Let us allow Mr. Masterson to proceed in his own obfuscatory way—I am sure he will edify us to our satisfaction."

Bat nodded a bow. "That's right. Hold your horses, gents, and I'll uncomplicate things. Now here's this kid, eighteen or so, tall, still on mother's milk and still growing. He hires himself out to a neighbor and gets a big basket and fills it full of little shoats."

"Shoats?" This was Wilson Mizner, himself a raconteur but at the same time an urban type who would not have known one end of a pitchfork from the other.

"Little pigs." Bat was patient. "Then he puts the basket on his head and walks around under the acorn trees and the shoats reach up and, say, don't they gobble those acorns. And of course, the taller he is the more acorns they can reach and the more acorns they eat the faster they fatten and the more neighbors hire 'im and the more money he makes. And that's called 'poling hogs.'"

The seven looked at each other. Then they looked at Bat, whose face was poker. George M. sat down slowly. "But what keeps the shoats in the basket? Why don't they jump out?"

Bat rose, frowning at the ignorance the question implied. "Because after he puts 'em in the basket, he pulls the tail of each and every one through a hole in the basket and puts a dob of mud around the end of it."

They gaped at him.

"The mud," said Runyon.

"In northwest Arkansas," said Cobb.

"Balls up easy," said Walker.

"Hard as a brick," said Mizner.

"Goodnight, gents," said Bat, and strolled away humming "Hello, Hawaii, How Are You?"

He stopped to tell Harry, the headwaiter, to put breakfast for everybody on his bill, but Harry shook his head.

"Sorry, Bat."

"Sorry?"

"Jack says no more."

"You don't mean it."

"You're up to three hundred."

"Chickenfeed."

"That's the limit. He says he's a sap if he takes any more of your tickets."

He was marching home under the rattling trestles of the Sixth Avenue elevated and madder than a wet hen when the back of his neck told him to stop, to turn. He stopped, turned. He waited until a Pierce-Arrow passed. There he was, the tall grim outlander in the slouch hat again, lugging the valise and following him on the opposite side of the street and also stopping. They stared. This time Bat had a strange sensation. It was as though they were locked in a silent struggle for recognition. It was as though each knew the other, or had known the other, but could not make the remotest connection between the man he had known, whether friend or enemy, and the man he now perceived. And after a minute Bat gave up the effort, tipped his hat to the stranger who was not, somehow, a stranger, and went on his solitary way.

His humble abode is a three-room apartment on the second floor of a brick-backed, brownstone-fronted row house numbered 300 on West 49th Street. Designed in the italianate style of the 1850's, these buildings, block upon block, were once fashionable one-family residences which typified midtown Manhattan from 14th Street north to Central Park; but now, gone to seed, they have been converted to rooming or apartment houses. They are a sore to the eye and a monotony to the mind. Signs sell music lessons from windows. A bottle of milk sours on a windowsill. Garbage cans lack lids. Cats vs. rats.

Bat begins to mount the steps.

Suddenly he is rushed from the rear. He tries to turn, is struck a blow to the side of the head which sends his derby sailing and sprawls him against the balustrade of the steps.

He pushes off and flails away with both fists. There are two men: the muscular mugs who work for Grogan at the race room.

He is no match. Th y are pros. Heaving lefts and rights the bastards batter him down on the steps again and go to work on his ribs.

He is frightened, hurt, furious.

Footfalls, someone galloping to his rescue, and the mugs are rolled onto him like barrels of beer.

Then they are off him and cursing and mixing it with somebody else, and beaten but unbowed Bat regains the perpendicular and ups with his dukes, and just as he spots the tall man who's been tailing him swinging away, one son-of-a-bitch does some fancy footwork and uppercuts Bat in a crude but effective manner, not unlike that of Battling Levinsky, the light-heavyweight titlist, and Mr. Masterson's bulb goes out.

He comes to. He lies supine on the steps. His jaw is still attached to his anatomy but his ribs ache like sin. He groans, elbows to a sit, and there beside him, hatless, gray mustache besmirched with blood, is the long drink of water who tried to help and for his pains had his own lights extinguished. He, too, has a gray roof. There is something faintly familiar about his features, which are intact—eyes deep-set, strong nose and iron jaw and big ears—but the face in sweet repose is scarcely grim. It is that of a gent getting on in years who, instead of fooling around at fisticuffs, ought to be in bed with a glass of warm milk.

He comes to, and with a haul on the balustrade sits up to groan.

"Thanks, pal," Bat mumbles. "I could've handled 'em myself, though."

"I noticed."

"Who the hell are you?"

"You don't know me?"

With a grunt and another groan, Bat gets to his feet. "Not from Adam."

"You've changed yourself."

"Who says?"

"I had to have a barkeep point you out tonight." The tall guy gets to his feet, rubs his right shoulder. "It's been a lot of years, Bat. A lot of water under the bridge."

Bat draws a sharp breath, which hurts his ribs. Suddenly he is rushed by recognition as he was just rushed from the rear by Grogan's crushers.

"My God, no," he mutters.

"Yes."

They stand on the flight of steps before 300 W. 49th Street in New York City at five o'clock of a dawning in the year 19 and 16. They stand as though each still disbelieves in the reality of the other. It has been twenty years. They were once friends to the bone. So they look at each other as though the world is flat and the moon is made of green cheese and Jesus H. Christ has just come back to earth.

William Barclay Masterson.

Wyatt Berry Stapp Earp.

"You're supposed to be in California."

"Trains run both ways."

"Why didn't you let me know?"

"I didn't let anybody know."

"Wyatt."

"That's right."

"I've never been gladder to see a guy in my whole life."

"You sure fixed me up a welcome."

They have a closer look at each other.

"You've put on some weight," says Bat, which is untrue but the only thing he can think of to say.

"You've lost some hair," says Wyatt, which is true and only a Wyatt would say it.

"Too many sharp turns under the sheets," says Bat.

They grin.

"Well, this is where I live, upstairs," says Bat. "And you, too, as long as you're in town. Let's go."

They retrieve hats and Wyatt's valise. Then, entering the building, the great gunfighters climb the stairs leaning on each other and puffing like steam engines going up a long grade.

The place of honor above the mantel of the tile fireplace was overwhelmed by the huge hind end of a bull buffalo with bold lettering on a brass plaque: "TO BAT MASTERSON, THE MAN WHO NEVER TURNED TAIL!"

On one wall was a banner: "IF MEN WILL SPIT, WOMEN WILL VOTE!"

On another wall was another banner: "DOWN WITH JOHN BARLEYCORN!"

"Committee out in Kansas sent me the buffalo ass and I'm proud of it," Bat panted. "The others are Emma's.

She's suffragette and W.C.T.U. You remember Emma Walters in Denver, in the burlesque at the Palace, song-and-dance, pretty as a picture. We've been married twenty-five years, doesn't seem possible. A sweet woman, Wyatt—worships the ground I walk on."

The rest of the living room was a coleslaw of chairs and tables and two horsehair sofas and lamps with frosted shades and tasseled satin pillows embroidered with such sentiments as "I Had A Swell Time At Coney Island!" and "God Bless Our Happy Home" and "Remember The Maine!" and pots of Boston ferns—all of these agglomerated on an Axminister carpet featuring faded pink and purple roses.

"Home sweet home," said Bat. "You still married to Josie?"

"Yup."

"Out in California, where d'you hang your hat?" Bat hung his own over a lampshade.

"We own a little place in Vidal. Summers we hitch up a wagon to some mules and camp out in the desert."

"Give me the bright lights."

"Thank God I'm a country boy." Wyatt was shucking his jacket and necktie. "I've been in New York two days. Three people tried to pick my pocket, a guy was going to sell me the Brooklyn Bridge, and tonight I get beaten up. What this town needs is a good marshal."

"I'd have you wash up," said Bat, "but you have to go through the bedroom to get to the bathroom and the missus is asleep."

"No need," said Wyatt. "I pissed on a Buick."

They undressed, backs to each other, shoving shoes under tables and spreading garments over the bric-a-brac like bushes.

"Even so, it's all here in New York," said Bat, taking up the thread of conversation as he took off a sock. "Wine, women, and song, and bigger and better than Dodge. And no damn cowboys to contend with. Oh, there's what they call 'gangsters' now, but they keep out of sight. You can walk down any street, day or night—"

"Like tonight?"

"Never happened before."

"Who were they?"

"Oh, a couple of mugs."

"You know 'em?"

"They work for a bookie."

"You owe money?"

"Wait'll I show you the sights!"

"You owe money?"

"You ever ridden on a subway?"

"Bat, you owe money?"

"Me? Not me. I'm no Vanderbilt, but they treat me handsome at the paper and I play a little poker and hit it big on a horse now and then—you recall, I was always lucky."

They turned. They stared.

"What the hell are those?" asked Bat. "They still wear longjohns out West?"

"What the hell are those?" asked Wyatt.

"BVD's—the latest thing."

"What the hell's going on out here?"

This was Mrs. Masterson, emerging from her boudoir in bathrobe and bare feet and blear eyes and rag curlers. She was no longer pretty as a picture.

"Ah, good morning, my love," said Bat. "Like you to meet an old friend of mine from the old days—he'll be our guest for a while. Emma, this is—er, uh—Mr. Dave Mather."

"Another Dodger," said Emma.

"We used to call him 'Mysterious Dave,'" said Bat in his BVD's.

"Pleased to make your acquaintance, ma'am," said Wyatt in his longjohns.

"What am I running—a flophouse?" asked Emma of no one in particular.

"The mystery was, how he made a living, heh-heh," said Bat.

"I'll bet," said she.

"You have a nice place here, Mrs. Masterson," said Wyatt.

"You have blood on your mustache, Mr. Mather," said Emma.

"My dear, we had the misfortune to collide with a lamppost," said Bat.

"Drunk," said his spouse.

"My ribs are stove in—have you got some balm you can apply?"

She went into the bedroom while Bat brought bedclothing from a closet. When she came back he lowered his BVD's from the top and she smeared his ribcage with goosegrease from a jar with one hand and held her nose with fingers of the other.

"Owww, be careful," he accused.

"Do you know what time it is?" she accused.

"Time for the arms of Morpheus," he smiled.

"But not for mine," said she. "I'm not bedding down with that stink. You sleep under the stars out here."

She went into the bedroom again and returned with a clothespin and a slopjar. She held up the clothespin. "Put this on your nose." She held up the slopjar. "Put this over your head. I won't have either of you traipsing back and forth with a bladderful of booze." She handed them to her husband and moved toward the bedroom. "When you get up—noon, I expect—I'll be gone."

"Where to?"

"Coney Island."

"Goodnight, Mrs. Masterson," said Wyatt.

"Coney Island?" asked Bat.

"I appreciate the hospitality," said Wyatt.

"That's right, Coney Island."

"What for?"

"To have a swell time."

They made beds of the horsehair sofas, only to discover that Wyatt's was too short because he was too long, so that his legs from the knees hung over the end. To remedy, they pushed a table to that end as an extender, and he could lay his lower legs on it.

"I introduced you as Dave Mather. Okeh?"

"Fine."

"You better be old Mysterious Dave from now on. The papers get wind of who you really are and you'll be a sensation. Crowds after you like a movie star." Bat turned out the lights and bumbled around in the dark and furniture until he found his sofa and sat down on the edge. "By the way, how long might you be here?"

"Depends."

Bat affixed the clothespin to his nose, took it off, and sniffed. "Damn goosegrease." He affixed it a second time. "I know one thing. You'll be with me, and after tonight, being with me won't be healthy. We better be heeled."

41

"Heeled? We wouldn't know the business end from the butt any more."

"We can still pull a trigger."

"Just about."

"Anyway, we better get permits tomorrow."

"Permits?"

"Have to have one here."

"Where'll we get the guns?"

"I've got a drawerful at the office—sell one to a sucker now and then. You might as well know—times have changed. This town's as tough as Dodge ever was. Maybe tougher."

Wyatt was silent.

"Well, goodnight, Wyatt."

"Goodnight, Bat."

Bat pushed some pillows around and lay down and tangled himself in a sheet. Wyatt was already stretched out, and appeared as well situated as a body could be with his pedal extremities eighteen inches higher than his head.

"I still can't believe it," Bat said, after a time. "Nobody else would either."

"What?"

"Wyatt Earp in New York City. The two of us together again."

Bat was right as rain. It was an incredible reunion. Friends for forty-four years, until tonight neither had seen or heard from the other in this new century. They had met as young men, almost as boys, hunting buffalo on the Salt Fork of the Arkansas in the winter of 1872–73; and if, in the granite

Wyatt, Bat found the first hero of his life, Wyatt probably found in Bat a kid brother more lickety-split than any of his own. Wyatt was dignified. Bat aspired to be. Wyatt cut the tongues out of hard cases with his fists, a skill Bat envied. Wyatt was greased lightning with a handgun. Bat resolved to jerk and fire till his finger fell off. Behind a big Sharp's rifle, Wyatt could figure carry and windage close enough to bring a buffalo down five times out of six at half a mile away. Bat would equal or bust. Wyatt was smart. "I think his outstanding quality was the nicety with which he gauged the effort and time for every move," Bat would one day write of him. "That, plus his absolute confidence in himself, gave him the edge over the run of men." As far as the callow Bat was concerned, the sooner he could raise his own crop of self-confidence the better.

Wyatt was honest, too, all wool and a yard wide, and there were damned slim pickings of such men on the plains. Most admirable of all, his hero had an iron rail for a spine. Years later, in the February 1907 issue of *Human Life*, Bat described Wyatt Earp as "absolutely destitute of physical fear." Bat the boy hoped he had been born brave—but supposing he hadn't, and guts were a commodity you could go out and get, he knew where to go. In the Wild West you wanted a fearless friend, one you could rely on in a tight spot, and now he had one. And so, he swore, would Wyatt.

The next twenty-five years tested the two to the utmost. Come day, come night, come snow, come dust, in silent street and ear-split saloon they backed each other's play. Up and down a frontier where whiskey was dear and life was cheap, each was ever-ready to sacrifice his own precious hide to save the other's. Even when events separated them, a wire from Wyatt put Bat, wherever he was, on the next train, and the reverse. They were marshals together in Dodge, with all the shit and shooting that implied, and deputy sheriffs of Ford County. They hit leather out of Tombstone after Luther King, who bushwhacked poor Bud Philpot off the seat during a stage robbery, and brought the murdering mother back. When competitors tried to steamroll Luke Short out of Dodge because he'd hired a lady piano player for the Long Branch, Bat and Wyatt and Charlie Bassett and Neal Brown and several others like-minded and armed came in from various points of the compass, appointed themselves a "Peace Commission," settled matters PDQ, had their picture taken for posterity, and paid for a piano tuner. In the late '80s the pair worked in cahoots at times as secret agents for Wells, Fargo, ranging even into Mexico when required. Later they found congenial employment and lodging in Denver. Bat presided over a faro layout at the Arcade, and Wyatt dealt from the top of the deck at the Central, but they commanded the same respect and lived in the same boardinghouse. It was there, in Denver, that their trail finally forked. Bat married and started a boxing club—no connection— and eventually lit out for New York City. Wyatt headed north, to the Dakotas after gold, and later to the Yukon. History did not record their farewell.

As boy buffalo hunters they met. As middle-aged men, and legends in their own time, they parted. About the breadth of their relationship, in terms of people and places, much was known; about its depth, little.

One fact was indisputable. In twenty-five years they had never thrown down on each other.

Bat's ribs hurt like blue blazes.

"Wyatt?"

"What?"

"You might as well know. I'm henpecked as hell."

"Me, too."

Bat came over, pulled up a chair, and sat down. "Something else. I'm stone broke. If John D. Rockefeller offered me one of his dimes, I'd grab it."

Wyatt sniffed, reached, detached the clothespin from Bat's nose, and affixed it to his own. "So am I," he said. "Broke."

"No. I heard you made a pile in Alaska."

"I did. Then I got shystered in real estate around San Diego. Then my claims in Nevada petered out. I'm living off Josie's money, and she never lets me forget it. That's why I'm here."

"Why?"

"I need a new stake. Bad."

"I'll be damned. So do I. I've had a long streak of bum luck. I'm in hock to a bookie up to my neck. That's why we got manhandled tonight. That's why we gotta carry iron from now on. The next time they won't be so gentle."

They were silent.

"I thought, New York City's where the money is and Bat is. If there's anybody I know who can take a pot with a pair of treys, it's Bat."

Bat detached the clothespin from Wyatt's nose and affixed it to his own. "Trust me. I'll think of something," he said, and went back to bed.

Under the goosegrease Bat's ribs began to burn, and one frond of a Boston fern dangled down far enough from a table to pester his forehead. He twisted and looked over through gray light and could see his friend's big feet on the end table outlined against a window.

"Wyatt?"

"What?"

"You comfortable?"

"As can be."

"Sorry about the sofa."

"No, I've got a cricky right shoulder—pain comes and goes. Arthritis."

"My legs cramp a lot. My feet get so cold I have to wear socks in bed. Poor circulation."

"Bat, how old are you?"

"None of your damn business. How old are you?"

"None of your damn business."

They were silent.

"We didn't even recognize each other," Bat said.

"A couple of old Colts," Wyatt said.

They were silent.

"Wyatt?"

Wyatt barely heard him over the early-morning roar of the city cranking up for another go-round. "What?"

"I'm glad you're here."

"Thanks."

"Damn glad."

"Wish I could say the same."

"That was bad tonight. You hadn't come along, I'd be in the hospital really bunged up."

"How much do you owe?"

"Over three thousand."

"My God."

"Emma doesn't know."

They were silent.

"You scared, Bat?"

"Me?"

Lucca let them cool their heels outside his office in the HQ at 300 Mulberry Street, and, while waiting, Bat described to Wyatt his beef with the NYPD. On detraining from Denver in '02, he'd been locked up by the cops immediately—the charge, having a hogleg on his hip. A friend he'd met in Kansas, the theatrical tycoon John Considine, Sr., went his bail, and he was immediately released, but the episode, rather than being embarrassing, turned out to be perfect press-agentry. The incarceration of W.B. Masterson, the mythical marshal who'd rammed law and order down the throat of the hinterlands, made every paper, and Bat was off to the celebrity races. It was the NYPD which was red in the face. They'd had it in for him ever since.

Anthony Lucca, the Commissioner, knew Bat, and Bat identified his companion as Mr. Dave Mather. "Friend of mine from Kansas, visiting our fair city for a few days."

"What can I do for you, Masterson?"

"Well, we'd like gun permits. Just temporary, two weeks maybe."

"No," said Lucca.

"You don't understand. Last night—"

"No," said Lucca.

"Last night we got roughed up bad, on 49th Street, right in front of my place."

"You saying our streets aren't safe?"

"Two mugs jumped us. It wasn't robbery, it was assault and battery and attempted mayhem and—"

"Not a chance." Commissioner Anthony Lucca had meat hands and a bullet head. He looked like a flatfoot who'd fought his way to the top from a Bowery beat. "You guys tamed the Wild West, didn't you? So take care of yourselves."

"Now listen—"

"Tell you what, though." Lucca grinned sarcasm. "You're not getting any younger, I'll give you protection. I'll put a man on you night and day—in uniform. Can't you see the papers? 'Police Protect Bat Masterson!' 'New York's Finest Shield Old Shootist!' Wait'll your pals see that. You'll be laughed out of town."

Bat scowled. "You'll laugh out of the other side of your face, Lucca. I've got friends."

"You got friends, I got the law."

"Thanks a lot."

"My pleasure."

"Come on, Wyatt—I mean Dave."

"You were bluffing," said Wyatt.

"The hell I was," said Bat. "We'll get permits. I've got friends in very high places."

They sat in Bat's *Morning Telegraph* office. Lewis had been introduced to Mr. Dave Mather, passed the time of day, and said so-long. Bat leaned back and deposited his shoes on his desk. Wyatt bit off the end of a cigar, crossed his legs, and lit up.

"Damn, my ribs are tender." Bat sucked on a Spud. "Wyatt, I've been thinking—the only way we can get rich quick is show business. Everybody's doing it."

They talked about that. Bill Cody was making a financial comeback with the Sells-Floto Circus even though he had to be hoisted into the saddle every show. Bat's friend William S. Hart was making moving pictures, in California, with Tom Ince and cleaning up. Frank James had done very well giving lectures decrying the life of crime. Bill Tilghman, a mutual friend from Dodge days who'd lately stopped in to say hello to Bat, had just made a moving picture called "The Passing of the Oklahoma Outlaws" and had, he said, high hopes for a big gross. As they talked, it developed that both of them had rejected fat offers to go on the road with the Buffalo Ranch Show and Wyatt, living not far from Los Angeles, was asked every other week to star in a film.

"Why don't you?" asked Bat.

"Just a fad, movie pictures," said Wyatt. "Not much future."

"Well, that leaves the stage. We could do a double— 'Masterson & Earp.'"

"'Earp & Masterson.'"

"Who says?"

"Sounds better."

"Either way, a few weeks on the circuit and we could bow out. I've got friends in vaudeville, too."

Wyatt pulled his chin. "Don't think I could, Bat. Make a fool of myself in front of people."

"For a thousand a week?"

"Oh. Well."

"Six weeks, six thousand."

"What'd we do?"

"Damifino. We can't shoot much any more, prob'ly, and we never did trick roping. There's a kid here now, in the Ziegfeld Midnight Frolic—Will Rogers. You should see him rope and crack wise at the same time. Anyway, all we've got is our reps and names—'Masterson & Earp.'"

"'Earp & Masterson.'"

"Either way, they're worth big bucks at the box office." Bat snapped his fingers. "Got it! I'll phone Eddie Foy! He'll put an act together for us!"

"Eddie Foy?"

"Sure. He's a name in this town, and he owes me. I saved his ass once—remember? I'll have to tell him who you are, but he'll keep it under his hat." Bat leaned, took the phone from the desk, and sat it in his lap. "By the way, Wyatt, do you fool around?"

Wyatt raised eyebrows.

Bat winked. "I mean, do you chase a skirt now and then?"

Wyatt clamped ethical teeth around his cigar. "I might. Now and then."

"Fine. I'll have Eddie fix us up with a couple of cuties."

"Eddie Foy here, too," said Wyatt, shaking his head. "I don't believe it."

"You didn't believe me either."

"I still don't."

They hopped the LIRR at Penn Station.

"Where we going?" Wyatt inquired.

"You'll see."

Then Bat hired a hack for Oyster Bay and gave directions to the driver so that Wyatt couldn't hear.

"Where we going now?"

"To see somebody."

"Who?"

"If I told you, you'd get cold feet."

"Goddammit."

"Trust me."

The hack clattered up hill and down dale and by salt marshes along the shore and stately homes facing the bay and swung into a graveled drive which circled up to a big house growing out of green lawns and guarded by great trees, its ground floor brick and ivy, its upper stories shingled mustard yellow, and the whole trimmed in rose pink. They pulled under a porte cochere, told the hackie to wait, climbed steps, crossed a spacious porch, and rang a turnbell. A colored man in a white jacket answered.

"Mr. Masterson and Mr. Mather," Bat announced.

"Yessuh, you expected. Come on in."

They entered and had a quick look-see through a doorway into a paneled hall huge enough to stack hay in, before they turned right and were led into a study with broad windows framing the crest of the hill before which the mansion was situated.

51

"He be right along," said the servant, and left them alone.

"Take off your hat!" hissed Bat, removing his.

"Why?"

"Take off your hat!"

Welcoming them from the walls were the heads of an Austrian boar, an Ethiopian gazelle, and some Congolese specimen with horns and a beard and a resigned expression. On the floor were the skins of a zebra and a lion. In between these on shelves were books, urns, pots, statuary, a ticking clock, and, below them, a zoo of leather couches and massive rocking chairs, the seats and backs of the latter swathed with the fleece of Rocky Mountain sheep. Suddenly he entered, crop-headed and barrel-chested, his eyes beaming behind thick lenses, his tusks flashing in that famous smile, striding at them as though he were charging out of a chute. He wore sweater, breeches, and cavalry boots.

"Bat, how grand to see you again!" The voice was unexpectedly thin and high-pitched, a reed rather than a horn.

Bat shook the extended hand. "Thank you, sir, a real pleasure to see you! I'd like you to meet my friend from Kansas, Mr. David Mather. Dave, the President."

Wyatt had gone white as a sheet.

"A pleasure to meet you, Mr. Mather!"

Wyatt had lockjaw. "Sir, Mr. Roosevelt, I, yes, well, say," he got out, and instead of his hand, shoved his slouch hat into the President's paw.

Theodore Roosevelt loved the West with heart and soul, and the men who made it equally. When, soon after his inauguration, he was informed that Bat Masterson was in New York, broke and arrested for concealing a firearm, he forthwith appointed him a deputy federal marshal and summoned him to Washington to swap lies about their youthful adventures beyond the wide Missouri. Bat later resigned the post and went to work for Lewis on the *Telegraph*, but from that first White House meeting, till Taft succeeded in 1909, a standing invitation stood. Bat took advantage. As the newspapers noted, he passed easily into the Oval Office while magnates and potentates twiddled their thumbs and waited their turn. President and plainsman made a mutual admiration society. Each saw in the other something of the man he might have been, and something of the man he would have liked to be.

TR assigned them a couch, pulled up a rocking chair, and for fifteen minutes shot the breeze with Bat while Wyatt, still in a state of shock, tried at least to look alert. Was the President of a mind to run against Wilson? Possibly, possibly not, it depended.

"Spoken like a true Mugwump!" added TR, rocking vigorously. "I don't like to be wishy-washy, never did, but it's all I can give you now, Bat."

"Well, if you do, Mr. President," Wyatt spoke up to their surprise, "you have two votes here."

"Thank you, Mr. Mather."

Who would the Republicans nominate?

"Hughes. He will resign from the Court, accept, and I will support him."

Would the U.S. get into the fracas in Europe one of these days?

"We must, Bat," said TR, rocking vigorously. "It is our duty—Germany has run amuck. And when we do, I will ask for command of a regiment of Westerners like the Rough Riders. We'll show the Kaiser a thing or two, by Godfrey!"

"Well, if you do, Mr. President," Wyatt spoke up to their surprise, "Bat and I volunteer here and now."

"Thank you, Mr. Mather. But aren't you two a little past the soldiering stage?" asked TR, grinning and ignoring his own age. He stopped rocking and sniffed. "What's that infernal smell?"

"Ahem." Bat cleared his throat. "It's prob'ly goose-grease, sir."

"Goosegrease?"

"I'm sorry. That's why we're here, Mr. President. I'll get right to it before we wear out our welcome. Last night two mugs jumped us and gave us a good beating. Emma—Mrs. Masterson—greased my ribs, but they're still sore. Dave here's staying with me a few days, and I tried this morning to get us gun permits for a couple weeks—to protect ourselves—but the NYPD says no cigar. D'you think you could help?"

TR launched himself from his chair. "Think I could? That's how I started out—President of the New York Police Board in '95! What's the Commissioner's name?"

His visitors rose. Wyatt put on his hat. "Lucca," Bat said. "Anthony Lucca."

"You'll hear from him shortly, mark my word."

TR walked them to the front door. "Delighted to see you again, Bat—and to meet you, Mr. Mather. You know who else I'd give my eye teeth to meet? That Earp fellow, Wyatt Earp. I'd like to have the straight of that shoot-out in Tombstone. Where is he now, Bat?"

"He lives in California, sir."

"Oh, yes, I think I've heard. I offered him a federal marshal's job in Arizona once, when I was in Washington, but he turned me down. I still have his letter somewhere— very well written and moving." He opened the door for them. "Good afternoon, gentlemen. And do drop in again, Bat—we'll talk till we run out of soap."

"I'll do that, sir."

"Bully!"

"Thank you, Mr. President," said Wyatt.

They shook hands. The door closed behind them.

But no sooner had they descended the steps to the hack than the door opened and Teddy Roosevelt marched down the steps to them. The sun sank in the west now, and mighty oaks and maples laid shade like compassionate hands upon the house.

"Bat, I hate to see you go. This country will never see your like again. And none of us is getting any younger." TR pulled a bandanna from a pocket and polished his glasses. They caught a glisten in his eyes. "You know, Bat, men like you and Earp will be legends someday. They'll write more books about you than any of us politicians— oh, the whoppers they'll invent!" He put on his glasses. "If you think you're famous now, wait till you're dead and gone!"

"I can wait, sir," smiled Bat.

"Likewise," said Wyatt.

"Right now," Bat reminded, "I'll settle for some Hart-ford hardware."

TR laughed, assured him he'd have it soon, saw them into the hack, and waved them on their way.

Going down the drive, Bat leaned out of the hack to look back.

"What?" Wyatt asked.

"I dunno," said Bat. "I got a queer feeling. That I won't ever see him again."

He continued to lean out of the hack, straining for a last sight of his friend. In the shadows under the porte cochere the twenty-sixth President of the United States seemed to diminish as he stood before Sagamore Hill, and when the hack turned onto the bay road he disappeared.

"**Left, one, two! Back, one, two! Right, one, two! Back—** Wyatt, what in hell's the matter?"

"I can't dance, goddammit!"

"It ain't a dance, goddammit!"

Emma was out, which was fortunate because they'd had to rearrange her furniture drastically to clear a little floor space. Wyatt sat stubbornly down on a sofa and put an elbow into a Boston fern.

"The audition's at four." Bat ran a finger round the neckline of his collarless shirt. "We've got two hours to rehearse. Eddie Foy worked out this step and got us a theater and we can't let him down. And I talked George Cohan into writing us a song—you realize what that'd cost us if we had to pay? George M. Cohan? And John Considine's catching our act!"

Wyatt had worked up such a sweat he'd taken off his shirt and was down to longjohns and suspenders.

Bat used the intermission. "All right now—do you know

any pieces by heart? What about 'The Face on The Barroom Floor'?"

"Nope."

"'Spartacus to The Gladiators'?"

"Nope."

"Anything?"

"Well, maybe," Wyatt allowed. "Mr. Roosevelt mentioned that letter I sent him when I said no to the marhsal's job. I recited it once, in San Francisco. I could do that, I expect."

"Fine and dandy. I'll do 'The Cowboy's Profession of Love.' The boys here get a kick out of that. What we've got to get down is the dance."

"You said it isn't a dance."

"It isn't, goddammit." Bat glared at him. "It's a shuffle!"

"I can't shuffle."

"Two steps left, back, two steps right, back, while we're doing the song."

"It's not dignified."

"Dignified!" Bat clapped a hand to his forehead and wandered amongst the furniture, then sat down opposite. "Wyatt, listen. You're here because you need dough. So do I—or any day now I'll be feeding the fishes in the East River. You know any better way to steal six thousand in six weeks?"

Wyatt chewed on his lower lip.

"Well?"

"Nope."

"Then trust me. The show must go on. Let's try it again."

Wyatt grudged off the sofa, Bat joined him, and they positioned themselves side by side, each with an arm about the other's waist.

"Just shuffle—two steps left, two back—here we go. One and two! One and two! Now right—one and two!

One and two! You're getting it! One and two! Hotsy-totsy! One and two! Hey, we'll knock 'em dead! One and two! We'll pack the Palace!"

They work in a large spotlight, center stage of the Belasco Theater, which is on the north side of 42nd Street west of Times Square adjacent to the Stuyvesant and Victoria. Wyatt runs through his letter, Bat his humorous recitation, and then the duo works with Al, the piano man, on the song-and-dance. Considine has not yet arrived, but Eddie Foy sits center aisle in the dark house offering suggestions.

Foy has had a string of his own hits on Broadway, from "Piff! Paff! Pouf!" to "The Earl and The Girl," but now, semiretired, he appears principally in other shows, in skits with his seven kids, such as "Fun With The Foys" and "Slumwhere In New York." He does indeed owe Bat. In 1878, while starting out as half of the hoofer team of Thompson & Foy, he was booked into Ben Springer's variety hall in Dodge City, and there one night, backstage, looked horrified into the muzzle of a six-gun. It belonged to Ben Thompson, a man-killer who was naturally mean and naturally drunk. Thompson would undoubtedly have nipped Eddie's career in the bud, and show biz would have been the lesser by Seven Little Foys, had not a friend of Ben's, young Deputy Marshal Masterson, sweet-talked him out of pulling the trigger.

John Considine shows up, greets those onstage, and seats himself a row to the rear of Foy. It was Considine, whom he'd met in Denver, who had bailed Bat out of the brig on the concealed-weapon charge, and Considine who'd just sold his theatrical empire to Marcus Loew for six million. A word from him over a drink or three at the Metropole was enough to put any performer's name in lights. He'd done as much for Charlie Chaplin and Marie Dressler.

"Curtain, Bat!" yodels Eddie.

"Going up!" Bat comes downstage. "Now Mr. Considine, this'll be rough, we haven't had much time to rehearse. Anyway, picture us in full Western rig, boots and guns and tin stars and all—we'll give 'em their money's worth. So here goes 'Masterson & Earp!' Okeh, Al, okeh, Wyatt."

He moves off, Al tickles the ivories into a fanfare, and Wyatt moves into the spot.

He freezes.

"'Howdy, folks!'" hisses Bat.

"Howdy, folks," Wyatt begins, and freezes.

"'My name is Wyatt Earp!'" hisses Bat.

"My name is Wyatt Earp. I've been marshal in Dodge City, Kansas, and Tombstone, Arizona—but you know all about that," he goes on in monotone. "But maybe you don't know this. Some years back, the President of the United States offered me the job of U.S. Marshal in Arizona, and I turned him down. Maybe you'd like to hear the letter I wrote him. This is how it went."

Al segues into "Poor Butterfly."

Wyatt freezes.

"'Dear Mr. Roosevelt!'" hisses Bat.

"'Dear Mr. Roosevelt. Thanks a heap for the offer, but I am going to say no. Sure, I'd like to work for you, and for this great country of ours. But it would be bloody work, I'm afraid. Arizona is still woolly, and if I were marshal, not a day would pass but some youngster would try me out on account of my reputation. I would be bait for grown-up kids who had fed on dime novels. I would have to kill or be killed—and you know which it would be. No sense to that. I have taken my guns off, and I don't ever want to put them on again. So let me spare the lives of these boys, Mr. President, and serve Old Glory in a private capacity. Thanking you again, I remain, Respectfully Yours, Wyatt Earp.'"

Al pounds the piano as Wyatt backs awkwardly out of the spot.

Silence in the Belasco.

Bat steps in. "He'll kill 'em with that, Mr. Considine! Now I'll do a recitation and pick up the tempo—okeh, Al."

Al starts a sprightly rendition of the popular "It's Tulip Time In Holland."

"Howdy, folks. I'm Bat Masterson, at your service! Now folks, picture a lonesome cowboy out on the prairie tending herd at night and writing a letter to his ladyfriend far, far away. He's pining for her, and here's what he might write. It's called 'The Cowboy's Profession of Love.'"

Bat removes his derby, claps it over his heart, and goes down on a knee.

"'Dearest: My love is stronger than the smell of coffee, patent butter, or the kick of a young cow. Sensations of exquisite joy go through me like chlorite of ant through an army cracker, and caper over my heart like young goats on a stable roof. I feel as if I could lift myself by my boot straps to the height of a church steeple, or like an old stage horse in a green pasture. As the mean purp hankers after sweet milk, so do I hanker after your presence. And as the goslin' swimmeth in the mud puddle, so do I swim in a sea of delightfulness when you are near me. My heart flops up and down like cellar doors in a country town; and if my love is not reciprocated, I will pine away and die like a poisoned bed-bug, and you can come and catch cold on my grave.'"

Al pounds the piano as Bat rises and takes a deep bow. "I'll have 'em rolling in the aisles with that, Mr. Considine! It's sure-fire!"

Silence in the Belasco.

"All right, now for the grand finale, Mr. Considine. You're gonna love this number—George M. Cohan wrote it for us—that's right, Cohan himself! It's called 'Mr. Earp & Mr. Masterson!' Okeh, Wyatt." His partner joins him in the spot. They position themselves side by side, derby tipped, slouch straightened. "Now remember, Wyatt, for God's sake," Bat backhands, "left, one two—back, one, two." He smiles. "Okeh, Al, let 'er rip!"

Al squints at the sheet and rinky-tinks an intro.

(TO PIANO ACCOMPANIMENT)

(SPOKEN SOLO)
"I'm Mr. Earp..."
(SPOKEN SOLO)
"I'm Mr. Masterson..."
(SUNG IN UNISON)
"We were faster than corn-plasters with a gun!
We stuck up for the law—
Beat the badmen to the draw—
Before the shootin' was begun—we won!"

(SPOKEN SOLO)
"I'm Mr. Earp..."
(SPOKEN SOLO)
"I'm Mr. Masterson..."
(SUNG IN UNISON)
"On the dodge from us they didn't run so far!
Made their play—got their fill—
Pushin' daisies on Boot Hill—
In the West we were the best—we wore a star!

61

We laid 'em low...
We hung 'em high...
Like the town of Tombstone we're too tough to
    die!"

(SPOKEN SOLO)
"I'm Wyatt Earp..."
(SPOKEN SOLO)
"I'm Bat Masterson..."
(SUNG IN UNISON,
SLOWLY, WITH FEELING, HATS OFF)
"We can't last—what's past is past—we're going
    gray.
Shed a tear upon our grave—
Tell your children we were brave—
When we're gone they'll carry on for the U.S.A...

Tell 'em how we made our stand—
Bringing JUSTICE to this land—
(UPTEMPO, HATS
HIGH, BIG FINISH)
Now we thank you, Ladies and Gents—give us a
    hand!"

Silence in the Belasco.

Eddie Foy appears out of the dark below the spot. "I'm
sorry, Bat. Sorry, Wyatt. Broken heart for every light on
Broadway, y'know."

"But where's Mr. Considine?" demands Bat.

"Oh, he pulled out, halfway through the song-and-
dance. It's not a bad turn, just needs some polish. But
cheer up—you're set for tonight with some lulus! You can
pick 'em up at the stage door of the New Amsterdam—
the Ginger Sisters!"

"The Ginger Sisters?" said Wyatt.

"Hot-diggety-dog!" said Bat.

Eddie Foy had gone, and they stood in the spotlight like two suitcase troupers who'd just got the hook and tickets to the next town.

"You were right," charged Bat. "You can't dance."

"You couldn't carry a tune in a bushel basket," charged Wyatt.

They glummed at each other.

"No use belly-aching," said Wyatt.

"Spilt milk," said Bat.

"Where do we go from here?"

"Damifino. Trust me—I'll think of something. What sweats me now is those permits. Not a damn word from Lucca."

"What sweats me is getting in the papers. Who-all'd you tell who I am?"

"Well, I had to tell Eddie, and he had to tell John Considine. Oh, and Cohan of course. But I asked him to ask everybody not to spill the beans. They won't. And that's only three people."

Al ambled blinking into the spot with paper and pencil.

"Thanks, Al," said Bat. "Want my autograph?"

"Got yours, Mr. Masterson."

He turned to Wyatt.

"Can I have yours, Mr. Earp?"

They lined up that night at the tail end of a line outside the stage door of the New Amsterdam on West 42nd. The line was composed of fashionable old ginks hugging big bouquets of roses. Bat muttered to Wyatt that these were so-called "Stagedoor Johnnies," adding that they should have thought of flowers, too. Wyatt said he couldn't afford flowers. Bat said he couldn't either. Then he had an idea, ordered Wyatt to hold place, and bucked the line through the door. Inside, he chinned with Pop, the doorman, who was reading a racing form, about a filly in the fourth tomorrow at Pimlico and inquired, incidentally, who the two gents first in line were waiting for. Pop clammed up. Bat fed him a fiver. Pop vouchsafed the info that the first two gents danced attendance upon Violet Spooney and Dilly Sheldon, both chorines in the cast. Bat said thanks, stepped outside, instructed Wyatt to look grim as hell, and led him along the line to face the two gents at the head, both of whom had chins as bearded as billygoats. He then addressed them as follows:

"You, sir, are waiting for Violet Spooney, are you not? And you, sir, are waiting for Dilly Sheldon, are you not?"

He glowered. Wyatt towered. The gents worked their chins as though chewing on tin cans.

"Gentlemen," said Bat with marital finality. "Miss Spooney happens to be my wife, and Miss Sheldon is this gentleman's wife. Just hand over those flowers and get the hell out of here," he growled, "or our attorneys will have you in court tomorrow morning for alienation of affections. Now you git!"

They got. Shaking and quaking, the old geezers got rid

of bouquets and decamped down the line as rapidly as their spavined limbs would take them, while Bat grinned at Wyatt and Wyatt gulped at the gall of it, after which they assumed places at the head of the line, each in possession of a dozen American Beauty roses.

You'd have known who they were if you had straw in your hair and took wooden nickels. In white high-button shoes they tripped through the stage door like twins, having poured themselves into identical long dresses of lavender silk cinched at the waist and ultradecolleté in front and back, with shawl collars of ecru lace covering their upper arms and white kid gloves their lower arms to the elbows. Before the first two gents in line they hesitated. Pearl chokers circled alabaster throats, while high over each head, its red hair piled and captured in a snood of gold mesh, waved a sensational ostrich plume, one sister's of pink, the other's of pale blue. It was practically the only way to tell them apart, for each had bee-sting lips painted vermilion, cheeks blushed by rouge, and eyelashes laden with mascara. If the two gents first in line did their damndest to look like ding-dong daddies, the young ladies had no wish whatever to dissemble. They were sweet patooties and proud of it. When they warbled "Ireland Must Be Heaven, For My Mother Came From There," strong men wept. When they chirped and undulated hips to "Aba Daba Honeymoon," they brought down the house. They could only be the Ginger Sisters.

"Mr. Masterson?" asked one.

Mr. Masterson removed his hat and inclined politely

from the waist. "At your service, ma'am," said he with a virile smile. "Just call me 'Bat.'"

"Mr. Earp?" asked the other. "The real, one-and-only, honest-to-golly Wyatt Earp?"

Mr. Earp glared at Mr. Masterson.

The white-jacketed arm of a waiter parts green velvet curtains and places before Wyatt a three-pound lobster. It seems to stare at him from the platter, and he returns the stare.

"What in hell is this?"

"That is a lobster," says Bat.

"What do you do with it? Wrassle it?"

"You eat it," says Bat. "Or take it home for a doorstop."

The girls go into gales of laughter while the waiter's arm is thrust thrice more through the curtains, bearing three more lobsters.

"We weren't born yesterday," says Bat to the girls. "Sure, you go by the Ginger Sisters on the stage—but what're your real names?"

"Do we really have to tell?" they appeal.

"Well, you know ours. Turn-about's fair play."

The arm parts the curtains and passes in, one by one, four boats of melted butter.

"Mine's Helen Troy."

"Mine's Juliet Bard."

"Enchanting," says Bat to Helen.

"Juliet," Wyatt repeats. The girls are seated in the center of the booth, Juliet beside him, Helen beside Bat. "How did you know I'm Wyatt Earp?"

"Eddie Foy told us—he had to. We don't go out with any old body."

"Old?"

"I mean nobodies."

The arm appears with four lobster crackers on a silver salver. Bat distributes.

"What're these?" asks Wyatt.

"Crackers. Get a good grip and use 'em like pliers. Start with the claws."

Wyatt watches attentively as the others commence to disassemble and devour the crustaceans. The arm removes a bucket of ice containing two empty Mumm's bottles. It reappears, bearing another bucket of ice containing two full bottles of Mumm's. Bat takes one and is about to pop the cork when Wyatt kicks him under the table and nods toward the curtains. The two men lean into the curtains and extrude their heads from the booth in order to hold a tête-à-tête.

"That's four lobsters and four bottles of champagne already and a private booth," says Wyatt. "What's all this going to cost?"

"A bagatelle," says Bat. "Anyway, it's on me, pal. I run a bill at Rector's."

Rector's is to the Gay White Way what Mrs. Astor's palace is to Fifth Avenue society. A long, low, yellow-brick building on Times Square between 43rd and 44th, its amazements include a giant illuminated griffin suspended from its facade and the first revolving door in the city— the latter contraption having caused Wyatt, who had never seen one, some difficulty with entrance. Inside, the establishment is elaborately decorated in green and gold, walled with mirrors from floor to ceiling, and lit by crystal chandeliers. On the second floor are seventy-five tables at which the hoi polloi are dumped. For the elite, one hundred tables and two private booths are reserved on the ground floor. And it is to this level that the bon ton of New York night life come after the theater in jewels and silks and soup-and-fish to be greeted by George Rector, to sip and to sup, to see and be seen, to crowd the place by midnight every night. Through these portals have regularly paraded such personages as Diamond Jim Brady, who bankrolled the restaurant in its beginning, and Lillian Russell, and Florenz Ziegfeld of "Follies" fame, and Anna Held, who took tub baths in milk, and the Floradora Girls, and Harry K. Thaw, who shot Stanford White over Evelyn Nesbit, and Charles Frohman and Richard Harding Davis, and O. Henry, whom few recognized, and young Billie Burke, and Victor Herbert, the composer who penned the immortal "I Want What I Want When I Want It," and, neither last nor least, the legs of Miss Frankie Bailey, which were unveiled nightly at Weber & Fields's Music Hall, legs adjudged by the stronger sex a national treasure and actually registered for copyright at the Library of Congress—not to overlook W.B. "Bat" Masterson, the Fearless Frontiersman, whose renown entitled him, on request, to a private booth.

Presently, in that booth, crackers crack and butter flies and bits of shell ricochet about like bullets.

"Are you married, Bat?" asks Helen Troy.

"Twice over," states Bat, popping the cork of the fourth bottle and pouring.

"Twice!"

"I have two Indian wives. Cheyenne. Brought 'em with me from the plains."

"I appreciate your honesty."

"Are you married, Mr. Earp?" asks Juliet Bard.

An arm parts the curtains and extends a menu and a pencil for Mr. Masterson's autograph, which he provides.

"I am," states Wyatt.

"Two Indian wives!" Helen exclaims, having thought about it.

"A chief can have two. And it's very convenient—I want what I want when I want it."

"But she's in California," adds Wyatt, "and a man gets mighty lonesome far from home."

Juliet changes the subject. "I love to dance. Do you do the Bunny Hug, Mr. Earp? The Turkey Trot?"

"No."

"How many men have you killed, Bat?" Helen inquiries. "If you don't mind my asking."

"If you don't mind my not telling."

"The Grizzly Bear?"

"No. But I do the Buffalo Wallow."

A waiter's arm is thrust through the curtains, removes the bucket and two empties, and replaces it with a bucket and two fulls. Wyatt kicks Bat under the table, and they put heads together outside.

"That's six bottles!" worries Wyatt.

"An investment!" responds Bat with a wicked wink. "What pippins!"

He withdraws, pops a cork, pours, and says to Helen, "But I will say this—there's twenty-three notches on my gun."

"Oooh, I'd love to see your gun!"

A droplet of melted butter rolls entrancingly into Juliet's cleavage.

"People want to buy it all the time."

"Buy it!"

"It's a collector's item."

"I read all about what happened in Tombstone, Arizona," Juliet informs Wyatt. "You know, you and your brothers up against those terrible men."

"Doc Holliday was there, too."

"What a battle that must have been!"

"It was O.K.," says Wyatt modestly.

They have annihilated the lobsters now, and are applying napkins prodigally while Bat pops the cork of the sixth bottle of Mumm's and pours.

"Yes, you must see my pistol," says he to Helen. "It's a very historical weapon."

Her upper lip still shimmers butter.

"Do you ever fire it any more?"

"Are you girls married?" Wyatt asks Juliet.

"Well, yes. But our husbands are in vaudeville—on the Pantages circuit. They're in Boston this week. I think."

Bat lights Helen's cigarette, which raises Wyatt's eyebrows. "Of course I fire it, my dear—whenever I can."

Juliet's hand is on Wyatt's knee.

"Vaudeville, you say." Bat takes an interest in all things theatrical. "What do they do?"

"Well, my husband is 'Beppo, the Sicilian Strongman,'" says Helen proudly. "He tears catalogues in two and bends iron bars with his bare hands."

Bat's hand is on Helen's thigh.

"Really?" Wyatt has always taken an interest in feats of strength.

An arm parts the curtains and extends a menu and a pencil for Mr. Masterson's autograph, which he provides.

"My husband has a dog act—'Carl's Canines,'" says Juliet. "They're the darlingest dogs!"

"Would they fight a badger?" asks Bat.

"The Buffalo Wallow?" asks Juliet, having thought about it.

"Two Indian wives!" exclaims Helen.

"Where do you girls hang your hats?" Wyatt inquires, his hand on Juliet's knee.

70

"We share an apartment in the West 50's," Helen confides.

A waiter's arm presents the bill, which Bat scans and requests a pencil.

"Would you like to see it?" Juliet suggests.

Instead of providing a pencil, the arm summons Bat beyond the curtains.

"Sure would," says Wyatt.

"Mr. Masterson, sir, sorry, but you can't sign," says the waiter.

"D'you know who I am?"

"I'm sorry, sir."

"Send George Rector over here."

"He's the one said so, Mr. Masterson. He says you pay up your whole bill from before, he'll run you another one."

Bat asks Wyatt to step outside the booth, then explains the situation. "I'm down to coffee-and-cake money. Can you take care of this?"

"How much?"

Bat hands him the bill.

"Sixty dollars and sixty cents!" Wyatt's aghast. "All I've got to get home on is a hundred-fifty!"

"You want to wash dishes?"

Wyatt pays up, adding after deliberation a dollar tip as Bat orders the waiter to inform George that, hoity-toity or not, a saloon is a saloon, and he will never patronize this one again.

Exeunt all, W.B. Masterson with lip curled, W.B.S. Earp in considerable dudgeon, and the Ginger Sisters in some disarray, their roses buttered, their ostrich plumes damped with Mumm's and drooping, their gold mesh snoods garnished with lobster shell.

Only to discover, as their hansom clops to a stop before an apartment house on West 58th, that their driver is Gas-House Sam, a notorious gyp, and that his price for the transportation is ten dollars.

"Ten dollars!" Wyatt barks. "Highway robbery!"

The horse retorts a Bronx cheer.

The Ginger Sisters giggle and sway up the steps, leaving a trail of rose petals.

"Two miles, ten bucks," says the hackie.

"You detoured us through Central Park!" accuses Bat.

Sam is adamant. "Ten bucks or I call a cop."

Bat takes Wyatt aside. "Pay 'im. I'll pay you back to-morrow. I told you, all this is an investment—in a few minutes the fun starts, and it'll be worth every cent, I guarantee it, pal. You ain't saddled up a big-city baby, you ain't saddled!"

"Where the hell you been!"

This from an enormous young man with pomaded hair and a swordpoint mustache and shoulders as wide as a barn and biceps as thick as Sears-Roebuck catalogues, wearing a striped tank top and tights, who is working out with barbells.

"Why are you home!"

This from Helen, ostensibly his wife, who has opened the door to the ratty living room of an apartment which, rather than being dark and conducive to romance, blazes with light.

"We closed in Boston," says Beppo, the Sicilian Strongman. "Thought we'd surprise you and—"

"We sure did!"

This from a tall slim young man in a boiled shirt and riding breeches and boots who stands ring-mastering four small dogs of indeterminate breed, but probably Pomeranians, with pink bows on their heads, who dash single file and leap one after another from a footstool to a table and up through a hoop on a standard and down to run in a circle to repeat the routine.

"Who the hell are these old poops?" Carl demands of Juliet, ostensibly his wife.

The Ginger Sisters' guests stand transfixed, mouths opening and closing like fish for air.

"Oh, these are our friends!" trills Helen. "Mr. Masterson and Mr. Earp!"

"What the hell they doing here!" growls Beppo, bending to pick up an iron bar.

"We . . . we . . . we just stopped by for a cup of . . . of . . . of cocoa!" manages Bat.

"Coffee!" Wyatt corrects.

"Coffee my ass!" cries Carl, snapping his fingers at his act.

Juliet attempts to untangle the contretemps. "You don't understand—this is the real Bat Masterson—and the real Wyatt Earp!"

"I don't give a shit if they're Buffalo Bill!" says Carl, picking up a telephone. "I'm calling a lawyer! We'll sue for alienation of affections! We'll take 'em for every cent they got!"

Round and round, up and over and through the hoop,

Carl's Canine's rush and commence to bark as they sense the drama rampant in the room.

"Oh, no, you can't do that!" yelps Bat.

"The hell I can't!"

"We gotta keep this out of the papers!"

"Headlines!"

"Mr. Earp's traveling incognito!"

Carl lifts the receiver from the hook.

"I'm a married man!" Wyatt protests.

"I have an aged mother!" Bat begs.

Helen and Juliet have slipped discreetly stage right into another room. Bat and Wyatt retreat toward the door.

"Get 'em, Bep!" cries Carl.

And with a bellow not unlike that of the male elk in rut, the Sicilian Strongman crashes across the room and, before his victims can find the doorknob, rams them both against the wall with an iron bar athwart their throats, then bends the bar into a V so that they are trapped, backs to the wall, their wind cut off. They struggle, but in vain. They turn blue in the face.

"What—can—we—do?" Bat chokes.

Carl comes to them, as do his dogs. The performing Pomeranians leap up at them and loudly bark. Carl shakes his fist in their blue faces while Beppo holds them in durance vile.

"You can pay up!" Carl snarls. "Try to make time with our wives while we're out of town, will you? Then you pay the price, you old goats! Let's have your wallets!"

"I'm—I'm—broke!" Bat gasps.

The Sicilian Strongman growls and bends the bar across their larynxes more brutally.

Bat rolls bulging eyes at Wyatt.

"But—he's—loaded!"

Up on the corner of Broadway and some street in the West 50's a Salvation Army band tootled "Nearer My God To Thee" in discordant hope, even at that late hour, of lassoing lost souls and bringing them into the fold.

Catching his wind, Bat sat on the curb before the Ginger Sisters' apartment house. Wyatt stood behind him, breathing like an old cayuse with the heaves. Noting a rose petal on the pavement, Bat picked it up and pressed it to his nostrils. He knew what was coming. It came. Wyatt stepped around him off the curb, loomed above him, took his slouch hat by the brim, and hurled it to the ground.

"Choused again, goddammit! I didn't come to this hellhole of a town to get plucked like a damn chicken!"

"We were set up, right from the start," gloomed Bat. "I should've known."

"You sure should—you're the city slicker! Why'd you tell 'em I was loaded?"

"Had to," said Bat, chin in hands. "Did you want to die in an iron necktie?"

Wyatt dusted his hat. "You're stretching our friendship out of shape," he warned.

Bat was thinking. "We had guns tonight, this wouldn't have happened. I can't figure out what's taking the President so long."

"Well, I'm cleaned. All I've got left is a return train ticket. What do we do now?"

Bat rose, rubbing his throat. "I'll think of something—trust me."

Wyatt put menacing hands on hips. "Bat, I don't ever want to hear you say that again."

Bat grasped his arm, suddenly, his attention riveted on something down the dark street. "Oh my God—look!"

Two men in leather caps. Grogan's muscular mugs have popped up from behind a flight of steps and start for them on the run. "Cheese it!" cries Bat.

They take off together, heading for the haven of Broadway. Wyatt falters.

"Shake a leg!" puffs Bat. "What's wrong?"

"Got a gimp knee!"

"You said your shoulder!"

"Knee, too!"

On the great gunfighters gallop, blowing and snorting, trying to get as near as they can, not to God but to the Salvation Army.

This time they were admitted to the office of the Com-missioner of the NYPD on the dot. Anthony Lucca sat behind his desk, fizzing like a fuse, and pointed at the permits on the corner of his desk. Bat picked them up.

"Much obliged, Commissioner," he smiled, passing one to Wyatt.

Lucca leaned forward and emplaced elbows on the desk and aimed two heavy-calibre fingers. "I want to tell you birds a thing or two. Mather, I don't know who you are and couldn't care less. But I know you, Masterson, and you listen. This is no bang-bang, birdshit cowtown thirty years ago and you're not marshaling any more. This is New York City and this is 1916. You behave yourselves. You be in bed early, both of you. You start shooting the lights out in our saloons or scaring our barflies half to death or plugging somebody to see if you can still do it and I'll have your ass in a Sing Sing sling."

"Wouldn't think of it," smiled Bat.

"Or a museum."

"Is that a fact?" smiled Bat.

"Or an old folks' home."

Bat bowed to Wyatt to precede him and, waving his permit at the Commissioner, toddled out humming "Be My Little Baby Bumble Bee."

"Jehu," said Wyatt. "Must be a lot of cowboys in town."

"I buy 'em," said Bat. "Ten bucks a throw, any pawnshop."

They were looking into the drawerful of Peacemakers in his desk at the *Telegraph*.

"Why d'you want so many?"

"I sell 'em. These tinhorn collectors come through every week. I've cut twenty-three notches in the grip and I lay it on the desk and tell 'em I won't part with it—I pull a long face and say that was the very gun killed Walker and Wagner after they did Ed in. Well, that's red pepper in the pee."

"They believe it?"

"One born every minute. Well, take your pick."

They laid out an assortment of iron and began hefting for balance and squinting down barrels and turning cylinders and trying trigger pull and ejector rods.

"Feels strange, don't it, handling these old thumbbusters again," Wyatt mused.

"Like old times."

They grinned at each other.

"This one'll do." Wyatt pushed the weapon under his belt.

"I'm all set." Bat belted his choice. "But we can't carry 'em this way, not in the city."

"How, then?"

"I know—shoulder holsters. We'll go down to Bannerman's downtown. They've got a line of everything, they can fit us special. Say, you ever used a shoulder holster?"

Wyatt shook his head. "No. Some did, though. Gamblers, mostly. But Hickok did, too, now and then. He told me so."

Bat was trying to ease the Colt out of and under his belt. It did not ease. "I must have put on a few pounds. I didn't know you knew Hickok."

"I didn't, not well. But I saw a lot of him the summer of '71, around Market Square in K.C.—the summer before I ran into you. I was just a kid, and he showed me some things."

Bat was interested. "You never told me. Hickok was a shooter, was he?"

"Sharp as ever I saw. I saw him drive a cork into a bottle at sixty feet. Split a bullet on the edge of a dime."

"Tricks."

"Try 'em."

Bat was piling the rest of the revolvers into his desk drawer. He winked. "Hickok couldn't sing and dance, though."

Wyatt was not amused. "Glad you mentioned it. I mean it, Bat, I've had a crawful. I didn't come clear across this country to sing or dance or drink four-dollar champagne or allemand left with your fancy chippies. I told you, I'm down to my train ticket. If I can't make a stake, that's one thing, but I'm not going home in a damn barrel."

"Stop fussing. I was worried about Grogan, that's all. Now I'm not. Now we've got guns, we'll get the money."

"Easy said. But where do we go from here?"

"Bannerman's. Let's ride."

Bat had hold of the doorknob when Wyatt said, "Wait a minute. You recollect Doc Holliday?"

"Sure."

"He was a lunger, you know—died in Colorado. I heard he asked for a glass of whiskey and drank it down. Then he said, 'This is funny,' and cashed in."

"So?"

"Well, that's funny, too, what you just said. Stop to think about it, that's the way it was back then. Still is, I guess."

"What?"

"Guns first, then the money."

They buttoned jackets over the pistols under their belts and left the newsroom and were passing through the reception area of the paper when Bat was pointed out by a clerk to, and accosted by, a matronly dame with a kid in tow.

"Oh, Mr. Masterson!" she gushed. "This is my son Waverly—he'd be thrilled to meet you!"

They stopped, Bat to offer a man's hand to the kid. "Howdy-do, Waverly."

Waverly might have been twelve, had an evil eye, and

a hand fresh out of the Fulton Fish Market.

"Would you give him your autograph, Mr. Masterson?" implored the dame. "He'd be thrilled!"

She provided paper, Bat his Parker, and while signing was put this question by the kid: "Did you really kill thirty-six men?"

Bat finished "W.B. Masterson" with a flourish, looked gravely at the kid, and lowered his voice. "Forty-six," he confided.

"Horsefeathers," said Waverly.

"Oh, thank you, thank you!" shrilled his ma, snatching the paper before the ink was dry. "We're ever, ever so grateful, aren't we, Waverly?"

"Aw, he's old," said the kid.

"My pleasure, ma'am," said Bat, tipping his hat and fighting the temptation to cauliflower the little turd's ear, and moving on with Wyatt.

They had just reached the front door when the room rang with a loud bang.

Mssrs. Earp and Masterson whirled, fumbling under jackets and hauling away at Peacemakers until, faces red as lobsters, they identified the cap-pistol Waverly waved at them.

"Har! Har! Har!" sniggered the squirt.

Wyatt wanted to walk to Bannerman's, which was located on lower Broadway at 10th Street. Bat was aghast. Walk forty blocks? Wyatt reminded him of his offer to show him, Wyatt, the sights. Bat suggested the subway, which had just been completed to downtown Manhattan, arguing that every out-of-towner must ride a subway. Wyatt reminded him that he had never hunted a hole in his, Wyatt's, life and was not about to. Bat suggested the Fifth Avenue bus, transport aboard which was available for ten cents. Wyatt reminded him that he, Wyatt, was broke. Bat suggested the nickel trolley car. Wyatt's response was in the negative. Bat suggested that a hike practically to the Panama Canal would be bad for his, Wyatt's, gimp knee. Wyatt reminded him that walking would be good for his, Bat's, cold feet and circulatory problems. Backed into a corner, Bat suggested they take a taxi, offering to pay the shot himself. Wyatt said Bat could ride and he would take shank's mare. He was an outdoors man and needed exercise and so, by all indications, did Bat, who was getting slow as a cow with a full bag. They looked hard at each other. Bat recalled: when Wyatt made up his mind on a matter, he was adamant as a Missouri mule. Wyatt recalled: Bat had always been as slippery as a hoop snake. Try to pin him down and he would slither this way and slather that and eventually stick his tail in his mouth and roll away out of sight. Bat suggested they toss a coin. Wyatt reminded him of his luck of late. Bat spat and got out a penny.

They hoofed the forty blocks, Bat on condition that they use a public conveyance on the return. The day was late April and lovely. Acting as guide, Bat pointed out to the tourist a variety of metropolitan attractions. Women beautiful enough to knock your eyes out, and gussied up in the height of fashion. Gents dressed ditto. The giant electric signs around Times Square advertising Uneeda Biscuits and C & C Ginger Ale and Studebaker autos. Streetsweepers in white uniforms picking roadapples. The Metropole Hotel, gone but not forgotten, in front of which Herman Rosenthal, the gambler-gangster, was mowed down, and for whose murder five men including a police lieutenant were fried in the electric chair. The choke of two-way traffic, a motley of hansom cabs, carriages, and bicycles, but mainly gas-powered now, sedans and touring cars and limousines and open-top buses. Policemen directing that traffic at the centers of intersections. A moving picture house showing "Hell's Hinges," the latest starring vehicle of Bat's pal William S. Hart. The green trees of Union Square. So-called "skyscrapers"—the Flatiron, the Metropolitan Life, the Singer, the Woolworth, etc. Saloons with side doors through which you could slip, if perishing of thirst, on Sundays. And finally, as they got downtown, the streets torn up to replace cobblestones with Belgian blocks.

"That's the trouble with New York," griped Bat the boulevardier. His dogs were killing him and the gun under his belt weighed a ton. "Always tearing down and putting up. I'm sick and tired of change—I like things to stay put. Getting on, I guess."

"Likewise." After thirty blocks Wyatt steamed along like the Staten Island ferry.

"I wonder what Dodge looks like now. I don't expect it's changed much."

"I dunno. Slept through it on the train."

"I'll take New York no matter what. Dodge is one burg I never want to see again."

"Likewise."

They were put into a private "fitting room," and what they found was that the shoulder holsters in stock at Bannerman's were designed for small-calibre, more compact weapons, the new automatics usually, not the old-time .45's they proposed to carry. The guy who helped them, however, a guy named Abel, said Bannerman's had work-men on the premises, and what they'd do, they'd remove the holsters on these rigs and sew on the right size taken off a pair of old-time cartridge belts. Said to make them-selves comfortable, the job could be done in a jiffy. Bat said fine, and when he brought back the merchandise, bring a few boxes of bullets, too.

"What's wrong with our belts?" Wyatt asked when Abel had gone.

"Too obvious. My friends'd fall down laughing. And I'd be stopped and bullyragged by every flatfoot on the force. I'd wear my permit out showing it. I told you—the NYPD's had it in for me a long time."

Wyatt considered, rearranging some splayed hairs in his mustache. "You sure we need iron at all?"

Bat set him straight on the birds and the bees. "Look. We got beaten up, didn't we? That was the first warning—pay up pronto, Masterson. Last night was supposed to be the second. If those crushers had caught up with us, we'd be in a hospital ward today, smelling flowers Lucca sent with his sympathy. They'd have used brass knuckles, or sapped us with lead. We'd have broken bones. Maybe we wouldn't even know who we were."

He took off his shoes and while massaging his feet tried to make it clear that the two mugs were only front men for Grogan, and Grogan was only a front man for some-body else—real, honest-to-God gangsters. They ran the gambling and the whore business and other sweet stuff in this town. They carried automatics in their armpits and called it "packing a rod." They put cement overcoats on people and let them see if they could swim in the East River. They had Irish and Jewish and Italian names but no faces. "I tell you, the cow-chasers we used to bash over the heads, the rustlers and train-robbers we ran around after from hell to breakfast, the mean two-gun sonsa-bitches we had to stand up to—they were small potatoes compared to the boys trying to collect from me. Well, yesterday they had the edge. Today they don't. Let 'em pack rods. We got artillery."

Abel brought in the goods. Shoulder straps were given final adjustments, the old Colts fitted into holsters made for them in the first place, coats were donned, and the buyers tried, looking a little foolish, a fast draw or two. Bat paid Abel with a fifty-dollar bill, which Wyatt noted, and while the salesman was gone for change, they loaded up the guns.

"I see you're flush," said Wyatt.

"Gives me a funny feeling, filling up one of these old boomers again."

"I see you're flush."

"Got paid today at the paper."

"Must be nice."

"The cat's whiskers. And not for the reason you think, Earp. My theory is, it takes money to make money. Okeh, I've got a hundred simoleons to spare—so tonight I'm gonna invest it."

"In what?"

"Pasteboards."

Wyatt put a testy pistol under his arm. "You mean I came three thousand miles to watch you play cards?"

Bat grinned. "A lot of ginks have paid for the privilege."

"You'll lose."

"Poker's my middle name. I'll run that hundred into a bundle."

"Unh-huh. I wonder how old you'll have to be before you learn."

"Learn?"

"How many peas you can hold on a knife."

84

Wyatt kept shifting in his seat. "Can't get used to this load on my left side."

"Be glad you got it."

"I never thought I'd see you hurrahed."

"I'm not. I was, but not now." Bat stuck a hand under his jacket. "Not with this, and you here, too."

"Don't depend on me. Half the man I was."

"Who isn't?"

Bat pulled on a Spud and cogitated. They had taken rear outside seats on the top deck of a Fifth Avenue omnibus—the only seats in which smoking was permitted—for the ride uptown so that Bat could have a coffin nail and Wyatt could rubberneck. As the bus started again and they neared St. Patrick's Cathedral, the smoker leaned to his friend's ear.

"Listen! Maybe we're half the men we were—okeh! Put your half and my half together and you've got one hell of an individual!"

"Till he comes up against a cap-pistol!"

"Anyway," said Will Irwin of the *Sun,* **"I thought what** Pershing said to the press was damned good. 'You may announce, gentlemen, that we have Pancho Villa surrounded on three sides.'"

"It won't play in Peoria," judged Pete Dailey, star comedian at the Music Hall.

"Generals don't have to be funny," said Runyon.

They were talking about Pershing's cavalry chase into Mexico after Villa, who had shot up several soldiers and civilians and the town of Columbus, New Mexico, in March.

"Jimmy here should be down there running the Army," said Bat, gesturing at James J. Johnston, pugilistic impresario known as "The Boy Bandit." "What would you say to the troops, Jimmy?"

"Stick out your hand and belt 'em out!"

Laughter.

"Hey, I just realized," said Runyon. "No wonder nobody's getting anywhere these days. We've got too many guys with J.J. initials. John J. Pershing, James J. Johnston, John J. McGraw—all losers."

Laughter at Johnston's and McGraw's expense. Jimmy wiped foam and a grin from his mouth. He'd just lost his lease of Madison Square Garden to Tex Rickard. McGraw looked glum. The Giants had gone three years without a pennant, and the sports scribes were turning out a lot of copy about his tenure as manager.

There were eight present—Bat, Runyon, Irwin, Dailey, Johnston, McGraw, William S. Hart, who was in town from the West Coast to hoopla his new movie, and Wyatt, who'd been introduced by Bat as "Mysterious Dave" Mather, a friend from Kansas, the mystery being how he made a living. They were bellied up to the bar in Toby's Slide, a watering-place at 50th and Seventh Avenue just west of the Garden Cabaret. You slid downstairs, everyone said, and crawled up, but it was popular with the nocturnal crowd because for 75¢ you could get a shot of good whiskey and a full tankard of Fidelio beer with which to neutralize the effect of the whiskey.

Pershing's running around in Chihuahua chasing Villa in vain, and Wilson calling out the National Guard to defend the border 'gainst invading hordes of Mexicans reminded Runyon of the immortal Masterson vs. Plunkett shoot-out in the Waldorf bar two years before—much damned ado about nothing much at all. Hart and Dailey and McGraw hadn't been there that night, so Runyon regaled them with a recap—Bat with gun hand in pocket calling Plunkett's bluff and the clientele smashing glassware in their haste to dive under tables or break down doors and Bat, later, when the smoke had cleared, pulling from his pocket in lieu of anything lethal a pack of cigarettes. After the punchline Bat took a bow and remarked that if panic was the point, he was reminded of a big night in the Lady Gay dance hall in Dodge in 1880.

A loud pause.

"Oh, no, not again," said Irwin.

"It's a true story," Bat insisted.

"Ring the bell," said Jimmy Johnston.

"Mather was there," said Bat. "He'll back me up."

"All right, suckers," said Runyon. "Let us put our faith in God and the grape. This round is on me."

Glasses and tankards were lined up for the barkeep, and when that worthy had done his chores the convivial crew assembled about Bat in various states of anticipation and inebriation.

Well, it seemed, he began, some quack from back East detrained at Dodge and commenced distributing cards which proclaimed his profession as "Physician-Phrenologist" specializing in "personal diseases" and his name as "Dr. Clapp." Well, this was a kumquat of an opportunity too ripe to pass up, so a few of the boys got together and formed a welcoming committee of "prominent citizens." They assured the quack that if there was any community in the West which had urgent need of a man who could handle "personal diseases," it sure as hell was Dodge City. And further, that they would provide him with a forum that very night, and an audience literally burning to hear his words and purchase his curatives. True to their oath, they sent the tidings forth, and by nightfall the coal-oil lamps were lit and the Lady Gay, a ramshackle wooden structure with saloon attached, was packed to the rafters with interested parties in the same condition as the lamps.

"Wyatt Earp and I were marshals then, and we took chairs on the platform to see that everything was orderly. I introduced Dr. Clapp as an angel of mercy sent to salve our sinners and he started his spiel. He got through a few lines when Luke McGlue hollered 'You lie!' That got things rolling. Now there was nobody named Luke McGlue, but whenever we pulled a stunt we picked somebody to do the dirty work and always called him Luke McGlue. Anyway, Earp and I loosened our guns and I told the mob to settle down and listen to what the world-famous medico had to say. So Clapp went on, using a lot of scientific lingo about the connection between the shape of the head and the health of the balls and pretty soon McGlue hollers 'You lie!' again. That set off a real commotion—you see, most of the audience wasn't in on the joke, they took Clapp seriously. Earp and I drew our guns and I told 'em to shut up, we meant business, we would kill the next loudmouth who interrupted the proceedings. Well, by this time Dr. Clapp is what you might call a hair unnerved, but he steps up to the platform again and does his best till suddenly Luke McGlue jumps up out of his seat and shouts, 'You lie, you son-of-a-bitch!'"

An intermission. Bat's timing was professional. He bent to the bar. With whiskey he lubricated his larynx, with beer his narrative powers.

"Make 'em laugh, make 'em cry, but above all—" said Dailey, "make 'em wait."

Bat was affronted. "Do I go on or don't I?"

"Hell, yes, go on!" cried Irwin.

"Play ball!" growled McGraw.

"Okeh," said Bat. "But I will kill the next loudmouth who interrupts the proceedings. Okeh, we were talking about panic, remember? Well, "son-of-a-bitch" was the signal. Earp and I cut loose and shot out the lamps, the place went dark as the pit, and I guess every drunk sober enough to find his gun went for it and started throwing lead. It was a real rannicaboo. Everybody headed for the exits at once. It was a wonder multitudes weren't shot or trampled to death. When we had some light again, there was poor Clapp under the table, praying and shaking like a leaf and his wallet was gone and his wig and practically everything but his pants and when we stood him up to see if he could walk he couldn't. But we weren't through with the faker yet. We said how sorry we were, and promised him to make amends for it the next day. We told him we'd get him a bigger audience, outdoors in broad daylight, and he'd do a land-office business—"

"Sorry, Mr. Masterson." It was the barkeep. "Telephone call for you. End of the bar, round the corner."

Bat frowned. "Excuse me, gents. Hate to leave you hanging—wait a minute, Dave here'll finish the story. Tell 'em about the next day, Dave."

He headed for the phone. The others waited upon Wyatt.

"Not much to tell," said he, with all the beans he had exhibited onstage at the Belasco. "Next day we pulled a big crowd in on Front Street and set up a box for the doc to speak from and waited for him to show. But he never did."

"Why not?" Johnston demanded.

"Because Bob Wright—a storekeeper—warned him to

get on a train and leave town, so he took the advice. Bob was in on it."

"On what?" Dailey demanded.

"The bomb."

"What bomb?" Irwin demanded.

Wyatt was uncomfortable. "The one we planted under the box."

"Well what in hell happened?" McGraw demanded.

"Nothing."

"Nothing!" cried Johnston. "Then what's the damn point?"

"Well, it was a good thing Clapp left town," said Wyatt. "We blew the bomb up anyway, and it had too much black powder in it. If he'd been on that box, parts of him wouldn't be down yet."

"Oh," said Johnston.

"Oh," said Irwin.

"Oh," said Dailey.

"Oh," said McGraw.

Wyatt leaned on the bar and studied his shot glass. Five of the other six leaned on the bar and studied theirs. Bill Hart, however, who knew more about the West than anyone present except Runyon, was studying the stranger from Kansas.

"Mather," he said.

Wyatt did not respond.

"Mather, who are you?" asked Hart.

Wyatt stared at him.

"I suspect a colored gentleman in the woodpile," said Hart. "There's something about you—I don't think your name is—"

"I've got it!" Damon Runyon banged his tankard on the bar for attention. He had scarcely listened to "Mysterious

Dave's" denouement. "Frien's, Romans, countrymen, lemme your ears!"

They lent.

"I've heard enough of this goddam Western buffalo shit! How's about we get revenge? How's about we give Masterson a stiff dose of his own Clapp?"

"Hear, hear!" cried the five.

Runyon might be in his cups, but even in theirs they knew that any idea bearing his by-line would be a lollapalooza. Damon Runyon's poems and columns in the *American* and short stories in *Collier's* and the *Saturday Evening Post* were up everyone's alley, even those of 42nd Street illiterates. He wore fifty-dollar shoes and monogrammed neckties. He was a born gambler. He bet on fights and horses and cubes and cards and ratting contests and elections and whether or not it would rain, take your pick. He would one day bet he could walk into the Stork Club in shirtsleeves, and win. He had already bet he would revisit the earth after death, and offered to let Satan hold the scratch.

"Aw right, aw right," he said. "We gotta set this up fast, before he gets back. Aw right, so he bluffed himself out of the Waldorf with a pack of smokes. Les' do 'er again, and this time do 'er right. This time les' put 'im up against somebody serious! Lessee what he does! I got a hundred dollars says he guts himself out of it again!"

They went for it like steers for salt—but how, when, where?

"Tomorrow night—the Knickerbocker Bar—midnight. Everybody spread the word—we want a full house." Runyon was improvising out loud. "I'll be responsible Bat's there. Now—the gunslinger walks in—lets everybody know he's from out West and he's got a big bloody bone to pick with Masterson—the place freezes—silence—they face each other—then the stranger orders Bat to slap leather or die yellow. Can you see Bat's face? Spuds won't save 'im this time! What a set-up!"

They seconded the motion with shots and suds.

"Just one catch," said Bill Hart. "Who do we get to play the heavy? He's gotta be the real McCoy or Bat'll laugh him out of there."

That stopped them. Then the cowboy star began staring at "Mysterious Dave" Mather, and the rest gave him a twice-over, too.

Wyatt shook his head. "He'd never believe me. We're friends from way back."

"Sure he would, goddammit!" cried Irwin. "Play drunk! Look murderous! Draw on 'im!"

Wyatt considered, then said, "Talk's cheap. You have to pay for whiskey."

Irwin was miffed. "What's that supposed to mean?"

"I don't even have a weapon," said Wyatt with a straight face. "I'm low on funds."

Runyon broke it up. "Oh, well, Christ on a crutch, yes." He pulled a roll, and peeled a double sawbuck onto the bar. "C'mon, you guys, everybody in twenty. Mr. Mather needs coffee-and-cake money—who doesn't?"

The rest began to pull and peel.

"Go 'head, take it, Mather. Tomorrow night midnight— the Knickerbocker. You be there with bells on—and a gun." Behind the lenses of his glasses, Damon Runyon's eyes were bright as his diamond cufflinks. He grinned up and down the bar. "Whassay, boys? Twenty bucks a throw for the greatest show in town!" He waved his roll. "Now for the side bets!"

"Tomorrow night, huh? Where?"

"The Knickerbocker."

"Oh, yeah, the bar." Bat was thinking. "All right, damn 'em. We'll give 'em a hell of a lot more than they've bargained for—I'll figure something out."

They had paused for a conference halfway up the stairs out of Toby's Slide.

"By the way," said Bat. "That telephone call was from Grogan. He wants to see me. Now."

"Strong-arm."

"I reckon."

"You going?"

"We're going."

"It's two in the morning. I'm tired."

"Shank of the evening." Bat took Wyatt's arm. "And listen, Wyatt, this is New York—don't get cute."

"Why go at all?"

"Knuckles Grogan pays the fiddler, friend, so he calls the tune."

"I don't dance."

They ease in through the dark cigar store on 43rd Street and through the swinging door into the race room and some long-shot surprises. The joint looks like after a raid. The bettors are gone, the bums have vamoosed, even Eddie the Cuff and the other bookies are conspicuous by their absence. Knuckles Grogan and the two muscular mugs are draped around behind the desks awaiting the bell. But you have to double-take the mugs because instead of caps and leather jackets they are all spruced up in pinstripe suits and felt fedoras and shoes up on the desks with spats. Bat comes out of his corner like a has-been with hungry kids.

"These your dogs, Grogan?" He scowls at the mugs. "Well, call 'em off. They tried to rough me up the other night—my friend here hadn't come along and reminded me of my age, I might have hurt 'em."

"Not my idea, Bat. The guy I work for."

"Rothstein."

"You said it, I didn't."

Grogan has the kind of voice he should have his adenoids out. He has a broken nose and he leans back in his chair, squeaking.

"Listen, Bat. You're into us for over three of the big ones. You got two days."

"Two days!"

"You're behind the eight-ball, Bat."

"I couldn't raise three grand in three weeks!"

The two bruisers rise from their chairs and circle the desks and a wary Wyatt and move across the room to take stands on either side of the swinging door. Grogan moves a big black Havana from one side of his mouth to the other.

"Two days," he says. "The other night was just a prelim. You don't cough up, you're gonna be in the main event."

Bat shoves up his hat. "What happened to Auntie Tan in the first at 'Gansett? I had fifty on the nose with Eddie."

"Finished fourth."

Sweat sparkles on Bat's forehead. "All right, listen. Here." He fishes in his pants and unfolds a bill on the desk. "I got paid yesterday. There's a hundred. That cleans me out. Put that on account and take the heat off. Gimme a week."

Grogan leaves it lay. "Sorry. Tell you what, though. There's a fight coming up—why don't you start touting McLaglen in the paper?"

"Your money's on the Sailor, huh?"

"We'll maybe forget the three grand."

"No deal. I don't do that. White'll massacre 'im."

Grogan salivas the Havana out of his mouth and produces a large silk handkerchief and blows his nose loud enough to wake a freighter in a fog off Sandy Hook. He tucks away the hanky and looks at the loser with sad, bloodhound eyes. "Sorry."

"Be reasonable."

"It's your funeral."

"Gimme a fair shake!"

"See you around, Bat."

Bat starts for the door, Wyatt after him. Suddenly they haul on the reins.

The two hoods have unbuttoned their pinstripe double-breasted coats and laid back the lapels to show off their armament. Each carries a snub-nose .38 automatic in a shoulder holster.

To their credit, the plainsmen appear to be unperturbed. Their jackets, too, are unbuttoned, their right hands free.

Bat had once written the following: "Never try to run a bluff with a six-gun. Many a man has been buried with his boots on because he foolishly tried to scare someone by reaching for his hardware. Always remember that a six-shooter is made to kill the other fellow with and for no other reason on earth. So always have your gun loaded and ready, and never reach for it unless you are in dead earnest and intend to kill the other fellow."

95

After a minute of silence, as though for the national anthem, Bat turns to Grogan.

"I don't scare, Knuckles. In my day I've stood up to redskins and cowhands too drunk to give a damn and guys really good with a gun. I don't scare."

"Rothstein don't either."

"You said it, I didn't."

That gets a smile out of Grogan. He nods at his nephews. "Okeh, let 'em go."

The Bruiser Brothers button up, smirking, and move aside. Bat and Wyatt mosey through the swinging door as though on the way to a tea dance at the Astor.

But as soon as they reach the cigar store Bat wraps an arm around the wooden Indian and hangs on. "Jesus," he breathes. "That was too close for comfort."

Wyatt doesn't hear. He has turned back through the door to face the foe again. Bat can hear his words to the hoods, and waits for the war to start.

"You better get permits for those poppers, boys. What d'you think this is—the Wild West?"

"Why taunt 'em?"

"I told you. I don't dance."

"Yeah? Who says I do?"

The great gunfighters conferred in whispers in the sanctuary of the cigar store.

"Goddammit," rued Bat, "I left the hundred on Grogan's desk—I could've run it up to a thousand at five-card. He'd have let me off the hook for a thou, maybe. My last chance—now I'm broke again."

"Speak for yourself. Your buddies back there at the saloon chipped in for a hundred twenty."

"For what?"

"My expenses. Tomorrow night."

"Eureka! Let's have it!"

"With your luck?"

"But I'm bound to—"

"Find me a game," said Wyatt.

"You!"

"I never lose."

Bat huffed and puffed, then knocked wood on the Indian's nose.

Poker was a popular pastime in the metropolis. Certain suites in the leading hotels were permanently reserved for the recreation, and there were other cloistered nooks too myriad to mention. The friendly game Bat located on this occasion was in progress in a back room at Doyle's Billiard Academy, an institution on 47th just off Broadway, and the dramatis personae at three ayem included Billy Jerome, Dumb Dan Morgan, Henry Blossom, and William J. Fallon. Bat knew them all, hence they were perfectly amenable to his companion from Kansas, "Mysterious Dave" Mather, sitting in. Fresh blood, they said, was always welcome. The game was five-card draw, open if you dared, raise if you could. Wyatt pulled up a chair. Bat hovered. The pace was leisurely, and there was desultory conversation about the shellacking the French were taking at Verdun. Morgan confided that he cared not a fig how many million Frogs were wiped out. He'd taken a welterweight and a light-heavyweight to Paris and been robbed by the ref both times, plus his rightful piece of the purse. Dumb Dan was a manager inclined to straight talk and crooked fights, his protégés being notorious for doing nose-dives when the price was right, and Bat had often cut him up in his column. The subject switched to Pershing's futile pursuit of Villa. Bat declared that ten thousand cavalry to catch one Mexican was crazy; given a three-man posse consisting of himself, Wyatt Earp, and Charlie Bassett, he'd have Pancho in the pokey in a week. Wyatt folded twice, won a hand on a pair of sevens, and lost one on two pair vs. a trio of ladies.

Fallon dealt. Wyatt opened on a pair of aces. Everyone stayed. Keeping a jack for a kicker—much to Bat's dismay behind him—Wyatt drew two cards and caught another ace and another jack. When he glimpsed the full house, aces over jacks, Bat had all he could do to keep from singing "Oh You Beautiful Doll!" at the top of his voice. Wyatt checked.

Henry Blossom opened the festivities. He was a playwright, but he hadn't had a hit since his *All For The Ladies* eked out a year at the Lyric in 1912. Since then, economically, he had run on his rep. He'd been bounced, the word was, in the company of a number of his checks, from membership in the Century Club.

Billy Jerome saw Blossom's bet.

Morgan raised.

Fallon stayed.

Wyatt raised.

Blossom folded.

Jerome stayed. William Jerome was a tunesmith and jack-of-all-theatrical-trades, having turned out "Sweet Rosie O'Grady," the books for several smash musical comedies, and many sketches for Eddie Foy. He was a faithful Masterson fan, and would one day pen a poetic farewell to Bat which Lewis would print on the front page of the *Telegraph*.

Morgan raised.

Fallon stayed.

Wyatt raised.

Jerome folded.

The pot was now of a scope to cause strong men to take stock. A wistful Blossom counted—there was just over six hundred dollars on the table.

Morgan raised.

It was now up to William J. Fallon, the original underworld "mouthpiece." He was a prominent criminal lawyer, having toiled in the vineyards of the courts for Herman Rosenthal until his client was gunned down at the Metropole. He had a high forehead and a Homburg. He looked again at the evidence in his hand, removed his chapeau, ran long white fingers through his long white hair, replaced the Homburg, and quit the case.

Two duellists remained—Dumb Dan Morgan and Earp, alias Mather.

Wyatt wagered his last twenty dollars.

Morgan saw the twenty and raised a hundred.

Wyatt sat like a wooden Indian until Bat forced him from his seat and steered him by the elbow into a corner of the room.

"We can't let him steal it!"

"He's maybe got the cards."

"The hell he has! Morgan's dumb! He's bluffing because he thinks you're a hayseed!"

Bat swung to the table, appealing to Jerome. "Billy, will you take my IOU for a hundred?"

Jerome reached for his wallet. "At your service, Bat."

"No." A stern Wyatt stepped back to the table. "I never borrow on a hand of cards."

"You're not borrowing, I am!" Bat was desperate. "I know! Wyatt's—I mean Dave's—got a one-way train ticket from New York to Los Angeles—turn it in and get a hundred at least! Will you take it, Morgan?"

Wyatt stared at Bat.

"You can't lose!" hissed Bat.

Dumb Dan was doubtful. Finally, under the silent pressure of his peers, he nodded. "Okeh. Maybe I'll go out and be in the movies. Let's see it on the table."

Wyatt continued to stare at Bat. Bat smiled at him. Wyatt found the ticket in an inside pocket, looked at it, placed it in the pot, and sat down again.

"I'll see you," he said to Morgan.

Fallon was on his feet.

So was Blossom.

Ditto Jerome.

Slowly, as though he were peeling tape from one of his gladiator's mitts, Dumb Dan peeled onto the table, card by card, four deuces.

By the third deuce Mr. Earp had risen, tipping over his chair. But by the second deuce, Mr. Masterson was no longer in attendance.

"He'll steal it, huh! He's bluffing, huh!"

"I thought he was!"

"Come out of there, goddamn you!"

In the manner of Samson pulling down the temple by a pillar, so Mr. Earp attempted to pull down Doyle's Billiard Academy by a toilet door.

"Come out and take your trimming!"

Mr. Masterson had taken refuge in a cubicle, and pains to lock the door.

"How'd I know he'd have four of a—"

"Every goddamn cent gone!"

Walls and floor of the pissoir were tiled, so that their voices volleyed and thundered.

"Now my ticket! I can't even go home, you tinhorn, stumblebum bastard!"

"I'll think of something! Trust me!"

At that, Mr. Earp went off like a black-powder bomb under a box. Hauling the Peacemaker from his armpit, he thrust it over the cubicle door, aiming low. Mr. Masterson's hands appeared on high.

"For God's sake, Wyatt—don't shoot! We can't pay for a crapper!"

Bat had gone to the *Telegraph* to whip out another column lambasting the White vs. McLaglen mismatch and pointing his trigger finger at a possible fix. Also, he'd told Wyatt he had to buy blanks and do some casting for the big show at the Knickerbocker Bar tonight. Under the buffalo butt, and wrapped in a quilt, his sidekick sat stiff as a board on a straight-backed chair, trusty Colt and holster hung over the back of the chair. Emma had done his laundry, and stood now at a board ironing his shirt and longjohns. She seemed to Wyatt to be less prickly today, even amiable almost, which meant, if he were any judge of horseflesh, that she wanted something.

"I can't thank you properly, ma'am."

"You were looking a little roady."

His curiosity was roused by what seemed to be an electric cord looped from the end of her flatiron across a table and up under a lampshade. "That's a new iron on me. Does it really run on juice?"

"The latest thingumajig—an electric flatiron. Plug it in anywhere long's you got an adapter. It was my present from Bat last Christmas. He claimed the Chinese laundry was robbing him blind." She turned the shirt collar. "Well, how d'you like New York?"

"Not much. It's wearing me down."

"That's not New York, that's Bat. He'll wear a body to the bone. I long ago gave up trying to traipse after him— I had to make a life of my own." She indicated the suffragette and W.C.T.U. posters. "So I did. Got my own causes and I'm my own person—as much as I can be." Out of habit she wet a finger with her tongue and touched it to the flat of the iron as though it had been heated on a wood-burning stove. "Can you imagine being married twenty-five years to a man who never grew up?" She finished the shirt and draped it over a chair. "Now fetch me your coat and trousers. They need a lick and a promise."

"I do appreciate it." Wyatt quilted into the bedroom. The woman was lonely. She liked to talk, seldom had anyone to talk to, and if she was agreeable to doing his domestics, he was agreeable to a listen.

"You did, though," she said through the door.

"Did what?"

"Grow up. You're not 'Mysterious Dave' Mather. You're Wyatt Earp, aren't you?"

He stood a moment in the bedroom, studying how to respond, then gathered up coat and pants, carried them back, and laid them on her board. "Yes, ma'am, I am," he admitted. "How did you know?"

"Woman's intuition. And Bat goes on about you so much. And I remember you from Denver, dimly. There was always something dangerous about you. Still is. Bat's mellowed. I don't notice you have. I expect you still attract trouble the way he attracts drinks."

"Now ma'am, I don't believe—"

"Don't tell me, Mr. Earp. You're in town a couple of days and already the both of you are carrying guns." She gave the ponderous weapon on the chair a sharp eye. "And I don't suppose either of you could hit the broad side of a barn if you were inside it with the door closed. Not any more." She shook her head. "Playing blood-and-thunder again, at your age. Shame. Oh, well, no fools like old fools."

Wyatt took to his chair.

"They your doing or Bat's? The guns."

Wyatt wrapped himself in his quilt.

"His probably. He's in a bind, isn't he?"

Wyatt set his jaw.

"It's money, isn't it?"

Wyatt sat like the Sphinx.

"I thought so." She went to work on his pants, separating the legs over the board at the crotch. "Well, I've been poker-poor and horse-poor all my married life, so I wouldn't know any difference."

Wyatt looked through her and through the brick wall behind her and all the way down to Times Square.

"I didn't go to Coney Island," she said, making small talk before she got around to the large. "The other day, I mean, after Bat made me so mad, dragging you in here like the cat."

"No?"

"I went to a matinee—I do a lot, the cheap seats. Once

103

a song-and-dance girl—you know. Anyway, I saw 'Stop! Look! Listen!' I'm crazy about Marion Davies."

After this irrelevance Emma Masterson pressed for a spell in silence. She wore a plain long skirt and a white blouse with leg-o'-mutton sleeves and looked very presentable. Spotting the slopjar under the sofa on which her guest made his bed, she pushed it out of sight with her shoe.

"Mr. Earp?"

"Ma'am?"

"Please take care of Bat, will you?"

"If I can."

"I couldn't bear to be a widow."

The windows were open to the morning, and garbagemen were banging cans around on 49th Street.

"I love him," she said unexpectedly. "And he loves me— in his way."

She creased the trousers and folded them neatly over a table and took up the coat.

"One thing I'm sure of," she said. "Bat's not a womanizer. I know he's true to me, as I have been to him. So at least I've got that."

"Yes, ma'am," said Wyatt.

They assemble in a small anteroom off the Knickerbocker lobby at a quarter of midnight: Masterson, Earp, and three hotel bellhops in snappy green uniforms with box caps braided in gold.

In a corner, away from Wyatt, Bat talks through the action with the bellhops. "Got that straight? You be outside

104

that bar door at midnight on the dot and ready to move in—okeh?"

"Yessir," they nod.

Just then there arrives a well-dressed elderly gent toting a black bag.

"Ah, here you are," Bat greets him. "Wyatt, here's our doc."

"Our doc?"

"You all clear, Doc?"

"I think so, Mr. Masterson."

Bat pep-talks the doc and the bellhops. "Now listen, everybody, spread out around the lobby and look natural. Do whatever you'd be doing—Doc, you read a newspaper, you three smash bags, hustle a dime, anything—but act natural, don't stick out like sore thumbs waiting. Then, afterwards, get back here fast, to this room, and I'll pay you off. Okeh?"

"Yessir," they nod.

Wyatt butts in. "Our doc?"

Bat ignores him. "Okeh, places everybody. And let's do it right the first time because that's the last time. So let's break a leg!"

Alone in the anteroom with Wyatt, Bat refers to his turnip. "Ten of. I'll go in there now and find Runyon and have a drink. I guaranteed him I'd be there. Now, you walk in at midnight on the nose. I'll be standing down the bar, hoisting one."

"What's this about a doc?"

"He's not a doc, he's an actor—unemployed. So I got

105

'im cheap through Eddie Foy. Now listen, Wyatt, to make this a real show, it's gotta be real."

"I don't think I can do it."

"Goddammit, you've gotta. They gave you a lot of dough, don't forget that."

"And you lost it."

"And we've got a packed house—I asked a bellhop. Now I've told you the play." Bat takes the tall man by both arms, pleading. "Listen, pretend. Pretend that bar's the Long Branch thirty years ago—remember? You're Clay Allison on the prod, you're drunk as a skunk, and you've been bragging around Dodge you're gonna lay Masterson low. You start out looking for me, you walk into the Long Branch, big as life and twice as ugly—and there I am. We look at each other and we know. Only one of us is gonna walk out of there. Pretend that's how it is."

Wyatt yawns. "Then can we go home and get some sleep? I can't take these late hours much longer."

"Sure thing. Now you can do this, Wyatt. You've got to, or my name's mud."

"You've got something up your sleeve. Why do we need a doc?"

It is eight minutes of midnight.

The Hotel Knickerbocker is situated at the corner of Broadway and 42nd. Night or day, its main bar, at the rear of the first-floor lobby, is one of the busiest Scotch-and-watering places in midtown. Men can be men here. Women, by unwritten rule, are scarce as hens' teeth. It is a room of calfskin wallets, rich tweed, friendly wagers, formal profanity, the aroma of bay rum, fine felt hats, the best bumbershoots, orderly digestion, and polite flatulence. The decor is eclectic—floor of mosaic tile, walls panelled in English oak, a high ceiling Flemish in design. Over the massive tables, on the wall opposite the mirrored bar, hang "Old King Cole," an expansive oil by Maxfield Parrish, and "Trophies of the Chase" by Frederic Remington. Attired in smart white jackets and white shirts with stiff collars and black bow ties, the staff of six bartenders, four scrubbers, and eight waiters is amiable and efficient.

It is seven minutes of midnight.

Efficient the staff must be this night in May, for the Knickerbocker Bar is mobbed with males. They have come in from touring honky-tonks and cruising cabarets. They have come in from upstairs saloons and downstairs dives, and from the theater, and from supper clubs such as Sherry's, Rector's, Maxim's, Delmonico's, and the Cafe des Beaux Arts. To be here on time they have missed deadlines, dropped dice, folded winning hands, bid adieu to bookies before placing bets, put down drinks undrained— a few have even excused themselves out of soft beds and hard embraces. They have come to see what Bat Masterson will do when confronted by "Mysterious Dave" Mather, a real Westerner with a real gun and, apparently, a real score to settle. Will he bluff and bluster? Will he try to pull the pack-of-Spuds trick a second time? Or will he, in the end, and to his everlasting humiliation, back down and beg for mercy?

It is six minutes of midnight.

The word has spread like wildfire. The show is SRO. Everyone who knows the great gunfighter by handshake has tried to be here. Some are sober. Some are soused. Every seat at every table is taken, and every inch between the tables and along the walls. The bar is lined two-deep, the brass rail sags, the air is infernal with cigar smoke, the bartenders bob, the waiters weave, the room rumbles with coughs, conviviality, and suspense. Eyes flick frequently to the clock over the bar. What makes this suspense tasty, almost sensual, is that it is safe. There will be no shooting. This is but a practical joke of classic proportions, conceived by Damon Runyon, and everyone will be "in" on it except the goat himself, W. B. Masterson, Esq. And so they wait, a hundred men and more, as children wait for treats or fireworks, itchy, breathless, jumping up and down inside. They watch the doorway, and the tardy clock. New Yorkers all, they are used to telling time, not to having time tell them. They wonder if he will appear. They wonder what the hell will happen.

It is five of midnight.

He appears.

The room stills.

He smiles, and affects surprise at the size of the house. He wears tonight a good gray worsted suit and a pearl derby cocked at an aggressive angle.

The rumble resumes. Eyes are averted from him, tongues loosed again so that he will not "catch on."

He strolls down the bar, shaking hands, waving, nodding, until he reaches Runyon and is handed a drink. Among those who gang about him are Billy Jerome, Hype Igoe, Alfred Henry Lewis, author and brother of W.E., his editor at the *Telegraph,* Charles Stoneham, and Gabby Dan McKetrick.

It is a minute after midnight.

Then two, then three.

When asked, the next day, what they talked about with Bat at the bar during this intermission, those near him will be unable to recall.

It is four minutes after midnight.

Eyes go to the clock again, then to the doorway, then to the clock. Only a few present have seen "Mysterious Dave" Mather in the flesh. Will he appear? If he does, will he have the moxie? Can he put on an act tough enough to put the fear of God in a fearless man? What in hell will happen?

It is five after midnight.

He appears.

The room stills.

They would curse out loud if they could. Mather is nothing much—a tall nondescript nobody of some years in a coat of one sort and trousers of another, with a slouch hatbrim pulled low over his eyes. He is a hick who does not even wear a gun at his hip.

The rumble resumes.

Mather moves slowly down the bar, and stops.

"Masterson."

He speaks, and no one pays him heed.

"Masterson!"

This salutation gets him absolute silence. Someone drops a pin, and the impact can be heard.

Bat steps out from his friends. A lane between the two men clears. They face each other at perhaps twenty paces.

Bat speaks easily. "Hello, Mather. Long time no see. What's on your mind?"

"You've run your bluff long enough, Masterson," is the gruff response. "I'm here to show you up for what you are."

Bat steps to the bar, puts down his glass, steps back into the lane. "You're drunk," he says.

Mather unbuttons his jacket, lays back the left side to reveal a shoulder holster from which protrudes the butt of an enormous relic Colt revolver.

"Draw," he says.

"Let's step outside," Bat suggests.

"Draw."

Bat unbuttons his jacket, lays back the left side to reveal a shoulder holster from which protrudes the butt of an enormous relic Colt revolver.

The crowd is gripped by general consternation. My God, Masterson is armed! Mather had to have a gun, a necessary prop—but Masterson, too, is armed!

"You'll regret this, Mather," warns Bat.

"I said draw!"

And on this injunction, Mather draws the revolver calmly from beneath his arm, points it upward, lets go a round into the Flemish ceiling, then calmly replaces the gun.

The report deafens. And as it roars from ceiling to floor, from mirror to wall, there begins in the room a mass movement as curious as it is understandable. Unlike the Masterson vs. Plunkett showdown at the Waldorf, which was memorable for panic on the part of those present, the reaction to this action is deliberate. Gentlemen slide very, very slowly from chairs under tables. Gentlemen lower themselves very, very slowly down the walls to the floor. Gentlemen along the bar move very, very slowly away to crouch and crawl over the gentlemen already under the tables. Bartenders and scrubbers sink very, very slowly from sight behind the bar. This, too, is panic, but of a slow-motion sophisticated sort.

They cannot conceive it. But a lethal weapon has indubitably been discharged in the Knickerbocker Bar. A nonentity when he walked through the door, the man nicknamed "Mysterious Dave" has become before their eyes a figure of grim face and great height and murderous intent. Masterson is armed and means business. The joke

110

has backfired, maybe mortally. Runyon has erred. The rest have made a fundamental miscalculation. What they are unwilling witness to, they realize too late, is the real thing. This may be Broadway in 1916, but it might as well be Front Street in 1876. This, literally, is kill or be killed. They have read the dime novels, they have seen the gun-and-gallop movies, and laughed. They laugh no longer. Souls shrivel. Hearts stop. Blood ices. Peckers shrink. Nuts dry.

"Draw, goddamn you!" Mather shouts.

Masterson draws and fires at Mather as Mather draws and fires at Masterson.

By a fraction of a second, Masterson is faster.

Mather is staggered, and toppling against the bar, fires a fusillade of shots at random.

Masterson fires at him again.

Mather hits the floor.

Masterson steps nearer, firing repeatedly, filling the fallen foe with lead.

THE END.

The room is a hell of smoke and echo.

Gentlemen crawl out from under tables and take unsteadily to their feet along the walls and rise from behind the bar and stare at the tragedy they have wrought. Mouths open and close in horror. There are groans of guilt. Tears flow freely.

Bat has gone to his victim, bends over him, then straightens. "Is there a doctor?" he appeals.

By fortunate coincidence, a well-dressed elderly gent toting a black bag walks through the doorway, spots the man prostrate on the tile, comes at once to him, kneels, conducts a brief examination, and rises to pronounce his verdict.

"He's gone."

111

Just then, by fortunate coincidence, three bellhops appear, and at the direction of the doctor, lug the late "Mysterious Dave" Mather out the door.

Raising his voice so that all may hear, Bat addresses the room in funereal tone. "I'm sorry," says he. "I had no choice. It was him or me." He shakes a sorrowful head. "He was a friend of mine once. He leaves a widow and six children in Kansas. Let's every one of us do what we can for them."

And removing his pearl derby, he moves to the far end of the room, extends the hat, and passes gravely along the ranks of mourners.

There is scarcely a dry eye in the house now, and by the time he is halfway to the lobby door, the derby is heaped high with currency. Damon Runyon, it is noted, has dropped in his entire roll.

Bat presses the hat tightly to his breast with one hand, while with the other he accepts additional offerings and stuffs them in the pockets of coat, vest, and pants.

He attains the door, turns, and for the last time speaks to the stricken throng.

"On behalf of his family, gentlemen, I thank you. Now let us bow our heads in prayer."

More than a hundred heads are bowed. In all the years of its existence, the Knickerbocker Bar has never known a moment as historic.

When it is over, Masterson has gone.

"What a show!" Bat chortles.

They toddle down West 49th Street on the way to 300,

Bat emptying his pockets and adding to a roll of bills big enough to choke a horse.

"How much did you pay those people?"

"Ten apiece for the hops, twenty for the doc—peanuts. Wyatt, you played it perfect—you oughta go on the stage!"

"Those friends of yours will ride you out of town on a rail."

"No they won't—they can take a joke. They'll keep this under their hats, though. Who wants the world to know how bad he's been conned?"

"I never fired blanks before—they sure are smoky."

Bat locates a last bill in a vest pocket and overlaps it. "What a wad! Must be four hundred bucks here, maybe more!"

"Fine. Hand it over."

"Hand it over!"

"What I said, pard. Remember, I left a wife and six kids in Kansas."

"Sure you did. Listen, we've got a stake now, and there's a horse at Pimlico tomorrow—"

"I mean it. Now I can buy a ticket home. I'm saddling up in the morning."

A bitter Bat halts. "That's right—leave me in the lurch."

An intractable Wyatt proceeds. "You're always in a lurch."

"But what in hell'll I do alone? You heard Grogan, you know the tight I'm in."

"Buy some more blanks."

Bat bounces after him, thinking, taking three steps to Wyatt's one. "Wait up. You're a hard man, Earp. Okeh, here's what I'll do. I've got a heart of gold. I'll split with you. Two hundred will get you home, and maybe two hundred will get me off the hook for a—Jesus!"

113

A bullet blows the derby from his bean.

A bullet buzzes Wyatt's ear.

They leg it behind the flight of steps leading into 300 West, then peek over the steps through the balustrades. Two doors down the dark street, two men rear up behind their flight of steps and blaze away again.

Grogan's pinstripe torpedoes.

Wyatt already has Peacemaker in hand. Bat draws his. They rise, squint, and squeeze triggers.

Clicks.

The Tombstone Terror and the Pride of Dodge City duck and gape at each other.

"Where's the bullets?" Wyatt hisses.

"I—I forgot 'em!"

"Forgot 'em!"

"I—I—when I loaded us with blanks—upstairs—for tonight—I forgot to bring bullets!"

"You lead-head dumbbell!"

The sound of running. They rise again to see. The gunmen run from their flight of steps to the next. Now they are within fifty feet of their targets.

They blast away again. Bat and Wyatt duck again. Slugs whang the balustrade above them, splintering chips, and ricochet along the curb.

Gunshots snap and pop in the canyon between the buildings. Lights wink on in apartment windows as residents take unkindly to the racket.

"We're goners!" Bat laments.

"If you get me killed, too!" Wyatt warns.

Full of confidence by the failure to return fire that their

antagonists are defenseless, the two torpedoes leave the cover of their steps and start to stalk their prey, crouching low, automatics at the ready. Closer they come, closer.

"Look!" Bat points.

Through the window of a second-floor apartment appear the head and shoulders of a woman, plus her arms, plus her hands, which hold a slopjar.

As Grogan's gansters prowl below, with unerring aim Emma Masterson dumps the slops.

The mugs are thoroughly doused. They sputter, cough, curse, and reel.

"Keno!" Bat hurrahs.

And while the assassins are thus diverted, with almost adolescent agility Mr. Earp and Mr. Masterson dart from behind the balustrade and skedaddle up the steps to safety.

So frazzled were they that they flopped down in chairs for a breather.

"What were you playing down there?" Emma Masterson stood in a doorway, her arms full of bedding. "Cops-and-robbers?"

The gentlemen declined comment.

"I didn't see you two shooting."

Bat scowled. "We forgot bullets."

His spouse smiled. "Probably just as well. Who were they?"

"I dunno."

"Welcome to New York, Mr. Mather. How long are you staying, by the way?"

"Leaving tomorrow, ma'am."

Bat hoisted his carcass and took off his coat. "Emma, now he's pulling up stakes, you might as well know. He isn't Dave Mather. Emma, meet the one and only Wyatt Earp."

"Wyatt Earp!" she exclaimed, giving a good imitation of Fanny Brice. "Wyatt Earp and Bat Masterson! And forgot their bullets! Good gravy!"

They looked sheepish. She plumped the bedding on a sofa. "Well, come to bed, Bat. You tuck in, too, Mr. Earp. Little boys need their sleep."

But he couldn't. He had much on his mind. And besides, he wasn't accustomed to hitting the hay before four in the morning, and it was not quite two ayem. Emma was dead to the world. He eased away from her and out of bed and went carefully into the living room where Wyatt was sawing wood on the sofa, lower legs laid up on the table. He nudged the sleeper's arm.

"Wyatt, you asleep?"

Wyatt's eyes flew open and his hand clutched something.

"What's that?"

"My wallet."

Before retiring, they had split the four hundred take.

"You mean you don't trust me?"

"I do not. What d'you want?"

"I can't sleep. I was thinking—nobody's taken a shot at me in twenty years."

"Me either."

"Funny. Here we put on a show at the Knickerbocker—

116

trying to kill each other—and a little while later, on my own street right in front of my own place, it was no damn show. Rubs me the wrong way."

"Likewise."

Bat, in his BVD's, pulled up a chair and sat near. "Rothstein'll kill me if he can, you know. That way he scares the shit out of everybody owes him dough. If he'll bump off Masterson, he'll bump off anybody—so pay up, boys, or else."

Wyatt closed his eyes.

"Funny," Bat mused. "In the old days, when I was in a fix I could set up a faro layout or go out and shoot a carload of hides. You, too. Times have caught up with us, I guess. Or passed us." He laid a hand on his ribs as though they were still sore. "You really going home tomorrow?"

Wyatt opened his eyes. "Yup."

"Why?"

"Well, for openers, I was pounded around good and then I got half-choked to death with an iron bar and then you lost all my money and my train ticket and made a damn fool of me in front of a lot of other damn fools and then I was nearly gunned down." Wyatt yawned. "We've run out of rope, Bat. This town's not big enough for both of us. I'm getting out."

Bat held his face and hands for a minute, then said in the same mournful tone he had tried out with such success on the congregation in the Knickerbocker Bar, "I'm a dead duck."

Wyatt closed his eyes.

It was after five and there was gray light through the windows and the clip-clop of a milkwagon down on 49th Street when Bat rushed into the living room and grabbed Wyatt's arm and Wyatt's eyes flew open and he clutched his wallet.

"Wyatt, the hell we have!"

"Have what?"

"Run out of rope! Listen—I couldn't sleep—I told you I'd think of something! Wyatt, it's time to pick our peaches!"

Wyatt heaved his lower legs off the table and sat up on the horsehair sofa in some disgruntlement. "What're you talking about?"

"I'm talking about how to get the big money we both need—enough to set you up so you won't have to live off Josie—enough to save my ass!" Bat babbled. "More than—enough to put us on Easy Street!"

Wyatt rubbed his eyes. "You're going to sell New York to the Indians."

"Goddammit, I mean it! All it'll take is that four hundred bucks and a few days out of town. You're leaving anyway, and I better make myself scarce. We'll go together, okeh? Today. This afternoon. How about it? What've we got to lose?"

"Four hundred bucks."

"An investment!"

"Lobsters."

"Forget that!"

Wyatt scratched an itch. "If this is another of your lame-brained—"

"This is a sure thing! Wyatt, this is the most sensational

118

son-of-a-bitch idea I ever had in my whole life!"

Wyatt looked askance at him, recalling Emma's remark about being married twenty-five years to a man who never grew up. He lay down again, curled up, covered himself with the quilt, and closed his eyes. "I'll sleep on it," he said.

"Unless we're too old," said Bat, and waited.

It worked. After a while Wyatt opened one eye. "Too old to what?"

"Hear the wolf howl."

The last time Bat had used his valise was on the trip from Denver to New York in '02. It was no wonder, then, that he had to grub for it under a pile of these and those at the bottom of the bedroom closet. He blew off the dust and slung it on the bed.

"Emma dear, I'm gonna be out of town for a few days."

This was news to her.

"Will you throw in a few things I might need?"

"Such as?"

"Oh, you know. Not much. Couple of shirts and ties, BVD's, socks, you know."

"Do you mind if I ask where?"

"Not if you don't mind my not saying."

"I have every right."

"Curiosity killed the cat."

"You're on the run, aren't you?"

"Yes and no." He was buttoning his vest. He winked at her. "Let's just say, honeybunch, that I seek a more salubrious clime. Anyway, I'll go by the office first and ask Lewis for a leave of absence. Then I'll be back, and Wyatt and I'll be gone geese."

"So will I."

"Do you mind my asking where?"

"A meeting." She opened a bureau drawer and began sorting out his things. "Where we sit around and spit and hate men."

"Bully. As TR says." He harnessed himself into his shoulder holster—which she noted—put on his jacket, surveyed himself in a mirror, pulled his wallet, came up behind her, and laid two twenties on the bureau top. "Here. You'll need some dough-re-mi. Buy yourself some pretties. See some shows."

She looked at the bills, then turned, suddenly, and flung her arms around his neck and drew him to her with such urgency that his breathing was obstructed by one of her rag curlers. "Oh, damn you, Bat," she said. "Why do men do things like this?"

"Nature of the beast."

"But you're gone even when you're here."

He put his arms about her bathrobe. "Em, you knew you married a sporting man. Give us a kiss."

She gave.

"Bat, will you please remember to wear socks in bed at night if you're cold?"

"Sure thing."

"How long'll you be gone?"

"A week, more or less."

She pulled back and looked him square in the eye and there was a tear or two in hers. "I love you, Bat."

"My slopjar sweetie."

She gave him another.

"One thing I'll tell you, cupcake." He was already adjusting his tie in the mirror over her shoulder. "When I get back, the Mastersons'll be in clover."

He was back from the *Telegraph* in an hour. Wyatt's bag was packed, and he held up his shoulder holster with its freight.

"We're leaving these, aren't we?"

"Oh, no. We're packing rods."

Wyatt frowned. "Now you listen. If you sucker me into any more—"

"Just till we're out of town."

Bat went into the bedroom and came out with his valise strapped. Wyatt had armed himself and put on his jacket and hat.

"You bid the lady of the house farewell, I presume, Mr. Earp."

"I did."

"What'd she say?"

"'Send me a picture postcard.' I hope you told her you're catching a train."

"I did."

"What'd she say?"

"'Toot-Toot, Tootsie, Goodbye.'" Bat went to the buffalo ass on the wall and gave the tail a twist for luck, then gave his grand salon a final gander, then grinned. "Choo-choo, here we come!"

Wyatt stood like a stone wall. With a finger he rearranged some splayed hairs in his mustache, thinking. "No. Something I want to attend to first."

"What?"

Wyatt told him.

Bat whistled alarm and said, slowly, "That would be very dangerous."

"They've got it coming."

"I don't care to get it going."

Wyatt smiled, then picked up his bag and headed for the door. "You'll come."

"The hell I will."

"Unless you're too old."

They mosey through the cigar store on 43rd Street, past the wooden Indian and through the swinging door into the race room. It is three-thirty in the afternoon and the three bookies behind desks, including Eddie the Cuff, are active on the phones and boys are chalking up results on the track boards and the room is crowded with lovers of horseflesh and vicarious participants in the "Sport of Kings." No one pays the new arrivals any attention as they shoulder through the crowd toward the billiard table at the rear of the room where, as they hoped, the two muscular-mugs pinstripe assassins are playing three-cushion, one bent over the table assaying an angle, the other watching him and chalking his cue tip. Mr. Earp moves up behind the one standing, Mr. Masterson behind the one bent. Mr. Masterson's eyes at this moment are a glittery gray, Mr. Earp's a cold and lethal blue. In a single motion Mr. Earp draws his Colt and raises it high. In a single motion Mr. Masterson draws his Colt and raises it high. Simultaneously they swing down and coldcock the mugs over the heads with the antique iron of the gunbarrels. The mugs fall forward over the table without a sound and commence to slide floorward in the manner of Texas cow-

122

hands. Before they hit the deck, however, Messrs. Earp and Masterson holster revolvers and catch the unconscious crushers and hoist them onto the table and lay them out on the felt as though on a slab in the morgue, faces up, arms at sides. This event has by now drawn the undivided attention of the entire room. Bookies hold the phones. Bettors and hangers-on stand where they are and goggle. Boys at the boards lean with arms asleep. Mr. Earp steps lively to the ball rack and returns to the table with two black eight-balls, one of which he hands to Mr. Masterson. Prying wide open the mouths of the seemingly moribund mugs, they ram the eight-balls in as they might apples into the mouths of roast holiday hogs, and stand back to approve their handiwork. Approving, the great gunfighters turn then and traverse the silent room with measured pace, Mr. Earp expressionless, Mr. Masterson nodding pleasantly to Eddie the Cuff, and disappear through the swinging door, Mr. Masterson humming the sprightly "Yacka Hula Hickey Dula."

They were fifteen minutes early. Bat wouldn't allow Wyatt with him when he bought the tickets—a round-trip for himself, one-way for Wyatt, upper Pullman berths. They went together then across the great Grand Central hall, giving Wyatt time for a good gawk, and down the marble stairs and onto the underground platform, where they still had ten minutes to twiddle their thumbs before boarding.

"Let's have my ticket."

"Not on your tintype," said Bat.

"I paid for it."

Being readied, the train hissed and chuffed and whined.

Porters and conductors and baggagemen and cleaning crews were on and off, on and off.

"I haven't been on a real train in a dog's age—Long Island doesn't count," said Bat. "Which side d'you mount from?"

"What train is this?"

"'The Wolverine.'"

"Where to?"

"If I told you, you might not go."

"What do we do when we get there?"

"I told you that, you sure as hell wouldn't."

"Then I sure as hell better not."

"We're gonna draw four deuces."

"Goodbye."

"Too late now."

"Does anybody else know where?"

"No. I told Lewis the same thing I told Em. The two of us are dropping out of sight a few days."

"What direction?"

"West."

Wyatt brightened. "That's more like it."

Bat put down his bag. "Wyatt, tell me something. How come you pulled out of the Arizona Territory after Tombstone?"

Wyatt clouded, and put down his bag. "They framed me—the politicians. If I'd stuck around, they'd have hung me for Stilwell."

"I thought so. The bastards. After all you and your brothers'd done to clean up the place." Bat tipped his hat to a Kewpie Doll tripping down the platform. "Did you ever hear how I left Denver?"

"Nope."

"I was having a drink by myself one morning at the opera house, the bar there, feeling pretty down in the

124

dumps. I'd lost my shirt bankrolling fights. Somebody snuck up behind me and stuck a gun in my ribs. It was Jim Marshall—you remember him. The mayor and chief of police hired him to come over from Cripple Creek and do the job—they didn't have the guts. Well, Marshall told me Denver was too up-to-date for an old gunhand like me. Said I had till that afternoon to get on a train. So I did. Sort of took the heart out of me. Came to New York."

Wyatt shook his head.

"What I'm saying is, they gave us the boot, Wyatt. We were like those old Colts in my desk. They used the hell out of us, then threw us away. No damn gratitude. Well, I was thinking about it last night—that's how I got this brainstorm. The West owes us. So if you have to know, that's what we're gonna do."

"What?"

"Collect."

Wyatt thought that over, then actually smiled. Bat grinned at him. It was good to be going away together again, loaded and ready for bear. It was like old times. On the shady side of middle age they might be, true, but they had been through thick and thin together, and nothing between them had changed, personally. Bat was a little thicker, Wyatt a little thinner, that was all.

People pushed along the platform. A whistle shrilled. Wyatt continued to smile, despite himself, and Bat to grin. The hiss and chuff and whine of the Wolverine excited them now. A bell clanged and a conductor cried "Booooooooooord!" and they swooped up their bags and almost kicked up their heels.

125

DODGE CITY, KANSAS

☆

The day does not dawn. The day of 3rd May is buried at birth under a crepe of cloud blacker than any in local memory. For those good folk abiding in and around Dodge City, Kansas, it is a day of portent. The Lord, they believe, is madder than a wet hen about sin or something. He may at any moment unleash His wrath in the form of lightning bolts, or floods, or tornadic winds, or quaking of the earth, or all of the above at once. But lo—at eleven o'clock in the morning there occurs a phenomenon the causes of which can only be divine. It is as though He's given things a think and changed His mind. It is as though a mighty hand passes o'er the heavens. The clouds roll back, as in ancient times the seas. A brilliant sun blesses His creation, set in a sky of benign blue. Some take note. A farmer, on his way to the elevator with a wagon of wheat, whoas his team in awe. Over a back fence, gossips lift their faces and their conversation to a higher plane. A minister, off on foot to console one of his flock, falls upon his knees in the middle of the street. Several of the faithful telephone the *Daily Globe* to inquire if the phenomenon heralds a Second Coming. Little do they know, or little reck. But if they do not, the Lord does. It is indeed a Second Coming, and He has made a miracle in its honor. For at 11:14 exactly, the "Scout" clangs and grinds to a stop at the Santa Fe station in Dodge City, and two gentlemen descend the steps of their car to take their legendary place once more upon the plains of Kansas. They are William Barclay Masterson and Wyatt Berry Stapp Earp.

The "Wolverine" of the New York Central had sped them overnight to Buffalo, across lower Ontario to Detroit, and on to the LaSalle Station in Chicago. Transferring to the Dearborn Station via taxi—it miffed Bat to discover Chicago as modern as New York in respect of taxis—they boarded the Santa Fe "Scout" and settled down to twenty-four hours and 789 miles of deluxe rail travel. Bat whiled away several evening hours, drinks, and dollars at cards in the club car. Wyatt looked thoughtful and read a *Police Gazette* and retired early.

They whistled through Joliet and Galesburg, Ill. They snored through Fort Madison, Iowa; K.C., Mo.; and K.C., Kansas. Between Topeka and Emporia they rolled out of their uppers and shaved, and it was then, blades stropped and faces lathered, hanging on to the sink with one hand and the razor with the other, that Wyatt popped the question.

"What time do we get off at Dodge?"

"How in hell did you—damn!"

The realization that Wyatt, if not way ahead of his plans, was at least keeping up, so startled Bat that he cut himself and had to apply alum liberally.

They breakfasted, paying, through the windows of the dining car, particular attention to Newton, and remembering. Neither in his youth had put in time or trouble in Newton, and though it was no more than a wide place in the road now, it had once been, like Abilene, Ellsworth, and Dodge, the end of the rail line, and hence a shoot-down-drag-out cowtown. It had been the spitting image, in fact, of Ellsworth, and it was in Ellsworth, in 1873, that Wyatt Earp first made his mark. He had buffaloed Ben Thompson—the same rare Ben who, had it not been for Bat's intercession, would have plugged poor Eddie Foy in Dodge five years later.

Thompson and his brother Bill were a sweet pair, and sweeter still when under the influence. They operated a floating faro bank and shot people. Bill's score was three, Ben's ten times that, give or take a defunct or two. In any case, they had Ellsworth treed that typical afternoon. Bill had run his score up to four by emptying both barrels of a shotgun into C.B. Whitney's, the marshal's, chest. The remainder of the peace force found a hole and pulled it in after them. An unarmed Wyatt Earp, pausing for a sarsaparilla on his unwitting way to Wichita, stood in the shade between Beebee's General Store and Brennan's Saloon, spectating, as Ben paraded up and down the plaza on drunken horseback, brandishing the aforesaid shotgun and fouling the air with profanity and daring the town to do anything about the murder. Standing with the stranger, looking him over and deciding him a likely lad, Mayor Jim Miller pinned a star on Wyatt's shirt and dared him to do something about it. Earp walked into Beebee's, borrowed a brace of persuaders, buckled them on, and stepped alone into the sunshine, hands easy at his hips. A sobered Bill had hit the trail by now, but, backing his play, Ben had a happy-go-lucky group of varmints including Cad Pierce, Neil Kane, and a troop of temperamental hair-trigger Texans. Walking steadily across the silent plaza toward Thompson, who kept him under his muzzles, Wyatt stopped at fifteen yards and told him to shit or get off the pot—to make his fight or throw down his gun. After a spine-tingling minute, and to the incredulity of the town, the county, the state, and the West, Thompson opted for the latter. Deputy Earp marched him to Judge V.B. Osborne's court, where he was fined a puny twenty-five dollars for disturbing the peace and banished to his hotel minus his weapons and aplomb, after which Wyatt returned his guns and sarsaparilla bottle to Beebee's and his star to the mayor.

On the spot, Miller offered him a cigar and the job of town marshal at a hundred a month.

"Looks to me Ellsworth values marshals at twenty-five dollars a head," said young Earp, drawing composed smoke. "So I don't figure the town's my size."

Two hours later the conductor came through calling, "Dodge! Dodge City!" They swung valises from the rack and moved down the aisle to be near the end of the car. If their hearts fluttered, if they got gooseflesh, if, in their systems, strange and almost juvenile juices began to flow again, they gave no indication. Perhaps, bending to peer through windows, they noted it an unusually gloomy morning. Perhaps they recalled the old joke about the cowboy and the conductor. When, in the roaring '70s, a cowboy up to the gills in alcohol was asked by the conductor for his ticket, he replied, "Don' have no ticket." "Well, where you goin'?" "Goin' t'hell." Whereupon the conductor held out his hand. "Gimme a dollar, then, and get off at Dodge."

At 11:14 exactly, the "Scout" clanged and ground to a stop at the Santa Fe station. Suddenly, miraculously, as though a mighty hand passed o'er the heavens, the clouds rolled back and a brilliant sun shone in a sky of benign blue. And at that very moment Mr. Earp and Mr. Masterson descended the steps of their car to take their legendary place once more upon the plains of Kansas.

They crossed the concrete platform.
They slowed, stopped, put down their bags.
Where in the name of God was Dodge City?
Where was dear old Front Street with its flies and chuckholes and dead cats and plank sidewalks, and hitching rails cribbed half through by the teeth of impoverished ponies, and jingling spurs and popping pistols and drunks laid out to dry? Where the loafers and landsharks lounging in the shade of the overhangs? Where the whiskey barrels filled with water in case of fire? Where the town well with its sign "The Carrying of Firearms Strictly Prohibited"?
They gaped instead at a paved thoroughfare and sidewalks and high-stepping pedestrians and electric lightpoles and one buggy and one wagon and a passel of coupes and touring cars and carryalls chugging along and not one solitary human being remotely resembling a cowboy or a cowhand or a cowpoke forked up on four legs.
Where was the unbroken line of wooden, weatherbeaten, false-fronted business and entertainment establishments? Where were the landmarks of their early lives—the Dodge House, Wright & Beverly's general merchandise emporium, the Delmonico restaurant, the Long Branch, the Alamo saloon and Occidental and Saratoga; Zimmermann's Guns, Hardware, and Tinware; the Blue Front Store, Coffins and Undertaker's Goods; the OK Clothing Store, Dieter & Lemley's Tonsorial Parlor?

133

They scowled instead at a solid wall of modern red-brick commercial buildings, the only exception one of white glazed brick surmounted by the only recognizable name—Drovers Bank of Dodge City—which used to be around the corner on Railroad Avenue.

At their rear, the "Scout" pulled out. They about-faced to the south, looking over the tracks which in their time had constituted the "deadline" across which the implements of murder and mayhem could not be carried north according to municipal ordinance. Where were the town calaboose, the Lady Gay, the Comique, the Varieties, the hurdy-gurdies, or whorehouses, the corrals, the cattle outfitting and supply stores, the shacks and sod huts and stacks of bones and hides?

They stared instead at block upon block of neat frame houses with flower gardens and nothing in the back yard, even a privy, but wash on the line and a shed for the Tin Lizzie.

"Progress," Wyatt intoned.

"Shit and shame," grumped Bat.

"You boys tourists?"

They swung around to meet the shifty eye of a very old gaffer who'd wheelchaired up behind them.

"You might say," said Bat. "We passed through a long time ago." He gestured. "What happened?"

"Front Street, y'mean? Hull shebang burned down in '85, so they built 'er up again. Brick. You dudes'll wanta see what they call a rep-li-ca, over yonder on the hill. Tourist 'traction."

He had a red nose and wore a battered ten-gallon and

134

from the smell of him imbibed that much daily.

"What else should we see?" Wyatt inquired.

"Ah, Boot Hill, likely, an' the Beeson Museum."

"Beeson? Chalk Beeson?"

"Himself."

"I'll be damned," said Wyatt. "Do you have a hotel?"

"O'Neal House."

"Where does a man get a drink?" Bat asked.

"He don't. Kansas gone temp'rance—that goddam Nation woman."

"A hell of a note. You lived around here long, Granddad?"

"Come out in '71. From Kentucky. Seen ever'thin' an' done ever'thin'. Caught a Cheyenne arrey in m'hip in '82 an' ain't been able since. Can't even stand up t'take a leak. But I knew 'em all—Earp, Masterson, Luke Short—all friends a mine."

"They were, huh?"

The gaffer shot a glance east and a glance west and lowered his wheeze. "Come close, boys."

They came close.

Methuselah reached into his shirt front and fumbled out an old Colt. "Either of you boys be inter-sted in a leetle sou-ven-eer? Belonged t'Bat Masterson—that's a fact. He give it t'me." He held it out butt first. "Lookee them notches! Seventeen!"

"I'll be damned," said Bat. "But I heard he bragged on twenty-three."

"He was a born liar, Bat was. Anyhow, seein's you boys are so sociable, you can have it cheap. Dirt. Fifty bucks."

"Fifty!" Bat protested.

"How 'bout forty?"

"I dunno," said Wyatt. "Only seventeen notches."

"Well, hell, cut yourself some more," argued the gaffer.

"I'll take thirty—I need the money. Otherwise I'd sell my stones 'fore I would this here gun."

"Tell you what, old-timer," said Bat. "You around the station most days?"

"Ever'day. Meet all the trains."

"Well, come time to leave Dodge, we'll get together. We just might do business."

"I'll be here." The pioneer shoved the souvenir into his shirt. "So long, pards. Watch out for them tourist 'tractions—don't b'lieve half you see an' less'n half you hear. We'll skin the ass off a greenhorn we get the chance't!"

From their arrival they had been under surveillance. They were about to smash their bags across Front Street, but there, at the curb, watching them approach, waited a buster in the pink of youth and a uniform and a badge, astride a motorcycle red as a fire engine and nearly as big as a horse.

"Good day, gents," said he.

"Yessir," said Bat.

"Welcome to Dodge."

"Thank you. You the marshal?"

"Oh we got no marshals any more. Peace Officer Harvey Wadsworth." And the buster put a hand to the broad brim of his hat and snapped off a salute. "At your service."

"Peace Officer?"

"What we're called nowadays. Ahem, well, gents, I hope you enjoy your stay with us and come back again. Be sure to see Boot Hill and the Beeson Museum and the replica of Old Front Street. Most folks find 'em mighty interesting."

He rattled off this Chamber-of-Commerce spiel and concluded with a smile which twinkled his baby blue eyes and dimpled his cherubic cheeks. His uniform, too, was baby blue, with gold piping and gold braid around his hat, and black leather boots shined as slick as a nigger's heel, and a flapped leather holster hung on his Sam Browne belt which housed some type of nickel-plated popgun.

Wyatt had looked him up and down. "You've been keeping an eye on us."

"Yes indeedy. I always come down to see the trains come in, see who gets off."

Bat was fascinated by his steed. "What kind of a cayuse you up on?"

That rang Harvey Wadsworth's bell. "Glad you asked. This here's an Indian Powerplus, fresh out of the crate." He caressed a handlebar as though it were an ear. "Lamps, generator, sireen, speedometer, and twenty-two horsepower. She'll do seventy-three-plus miles an hour—factory guaranteed. I tell you, they don't even have these in New York City!"

"I'll be damned," said Bat. "You must catch a bunch of rustlers at that rate."

"Rustlers, ha. Speeders—that's about all the crime we got."

"I'll be damned—speeders," said Bat. "By the way, where does a man get a drink around here?"

"Sorry," said Wadsworth. "We been dry as a bone for years. Closed the last saloon in Dodge in 1903. Oh, you can get booze in a pharmacy—but only for medicinal purposes."

"Hmmm," Bat reflected. "Must be why I'm feeling so poorly lately. Well, thanks a lot, Officer."

"You're entirely welcome. Say, I didn't catch your names, gents."

Bat opened his mouth. He was about to say Enrico Caruso and William Randolph Hearst, but Wyatt beat him to it. "I'm Wyatt Earp. This is Bat Masterson."

Harvey Wadsworth's grin spread halfway round his head. "Earp and Masterson again, huh? Funny how you gents keep showing up all the time. Well, nice to know you're here. I get in a pinch, I'll holler for your six-guns!"

The young minion of the law snapped them another salute, booted the big Indian into noisy life, and galloped off in a cloud of exhaust.

Bat was angry. "Why in hell would you tell 'im our names!"

Wyatt picked up his valise. "Use your head. Those are the only names he'd never believe."

They ran into the same identity oddity while checking into the O'Neal House. Wyatt appropriated the pen before Bat could, and signed the register for both of them, after which the whippersnapper desk clerk turned the book for a look.

"Earp and Masterson again, huh? Our best customers— why, I bet you two sign in a hundred times a year!" If the peace officer's grin had been innocently cynical, the clerk's leer was downright decadent. "Bring along your wives, too, sometimes—Mr. and Mrs. Earp, Mr. and Mrs. Masterson—overnights mostly."

"Izzatso?" said Bat.

"How long since you've been taken out to the woodshed?" Wyatt asked.

The clerk colored. "Well, say, I'm sorry, gents. No offense. Welcome to Dodge and enjoy your stay. And while you're here, be sure to see Old Front Street and the Beeson Museum and Boot Hill. Everybody does and everybody's glad they did."

"Wouldn't miss 'em," said Bat, hitting the spittoon with his first shot.

They took adjoining rooms and naps because the train had tired them, and while they were washing up in the bowls preparatory to going out, Wyatt spoke to Bat through the open transom over the door between their rooms, which was locked.

"Can you hear me?"

"Easy. What's on your mind?"

"What's on yours? You've been playing your cards close to the vest. What's next?"

"Old Front Street."

"You know what I mean."

Bat paused, towel at his cheeks. He was as well acquainted with Wyatt Earp as anyone could be. To his knowledge, Wyatt had cottoned to only two males not related to him in his lifetime—himself and Doc Holliday. He was a loner. He was taciturn and immutable. Get on his right side and he would travel with you to Timbuctoo or Kansas. Cross him, even to this day, and you walked into a buzz saw. From what Bat had seen of him in New York, he had altered little. Rather than mellowing him, the years had sharpened his edge.

"I'll tell you," Bat said. "But I have to pick my time."

"Why?"

"You might get mad. And you're heeled."

"Sheepshit."

"If that isn't a sad, son-of-a-bitching sight," Bat groaned.

"Sickening," Wyatt growled.

They had paid four bits apiece to a girl in a booth, then climbed steps to stand at one end of historic Old Front Street—the so-called "replica" thereof. Oh, there was a block-long stretch of wooden, one-story, false-fronted business and entertainments—the Delmonico restaurant, the Long Branch, a grocery store, dry goods and clothing, barber shop, gunsmith's, a bank, etc. But they were dolled up in new paint and fancy lettering and the plank sidewalk looked as though it had just been laid. If this was history, a three-dollar bill was legal tender. If this was supposed to be a fair reproduction, Big Nose Kate was the Queen of Sheba. If this bore even the remotest resemblance to the main Dodge drag in the good old days, a turd was a chocolate eclair.

Silently, hands in pockets, they clumped along the planks. Inside, the stores fobbed off a wide assortment of cheap doodads on a gullible public. They entered the Long Branch. Oh, it had a bar and a mirror and a buffalo head and tintypes of forgotten frontier reprobates on the walls, but all the costumed lady behind the bar could sell them was soda pop or some fizz called "Green River."

They took paper cups of the fizz outside and sat down in chairs under the overhang and sipped and cussed and hurled the damn Green River away and propped back against the wall and sat for some time in silence, chewing cuds of sadness and resentment. They felt like ghosts come back to find the graveyard gone.

140

"Girl in the booth said the suckers start coming next month," said Bat.

"Um," said Wyatt.

"They'll run a hundred thousand of 'em through here in a summer, at four bits a head. You add that up."

"Um."

"They've got a stagecoach and sell rides. And every couple hours they put on a shoot-out, a bunch of drip-nose high school kids all dressed up. Blanks. Bat Masterson and Wyatt Earp versus a gang of Texas bad guys. Lotsa noise and ketchup and bodies. Guess who wins."

"Um."

A waning afternoon sun warmed them. No one else was about. A bit of a breeze from Colorado blew along Old Front Street, bemoaning the past and chiding the present. From their height the two gents propped back in chairs overlooked the new Front Street below and to the left, and the paved area that had once been a dusty plaza bisected by the tracks of the Santa Fe. It was in this plaza, not so long ago it seemed, that Bat had jumped from a train into a bushwhack. By the time he could jerk his gun he was being fired at from differing points of the compass by A.J. Peacock, Al Updegraff, et al. By the time it was over, Updegraff had a slug in the lung, ten pounds of lead had been expended, and Bat had paid a fine of eight dollars for "unlawfully and feloniously discharging a pistol in the streets." It was in this plaza, a year or so ago it seemed, that Wyatt got the shotgun drop on Shanghai Pierce, the cattle baron, and his trailhands, and marched them before the magistrate.

And it was in this plaza, only yesterday it seemed, Bat and Charlie Bassett backing his play, that Wyatt earned more immortality by bringing Clay Allison to heel. Allison had shot down six marshals and sheriffs. Allison rode horses into saloons stark naked and redecorated them with cartridges. Allison had drawn and killed a man while dining in a restaurant and finished his repast at leisure, smoking revolver on the table and corpse on the carpet. Allison was so touchy that once, in Las Animas, New Mexico, when he had a toothache and a dentist pulled the wrong molar, Allison tied the poor devil in his own chair and with his own forceps extracted every chopper in the dentist's head. But in the end it was the intrepid Earp who walked up to Allison, shoved a forty-five in his ribs, and ran him out of Dodge with tail between legs and the fear of God up his ass.

"Wyatt," said Bat, "I've been thinking. I started thinking in New York—that's how I got this idea."

Wyatt waited.

"But before I tell you the idea, I want to say how I feel. I'm more sure I'm right now—now we're here—than I was then. I mean, sure I'm right."

Wyatt waited.

"But I don't want you to get riled till you hear me out. That is, how I feel, what I'm thinking."

Wyatt reached into his jacket and slid the Colt from his armpit and laid it in his lap. This made Bat uncomfortable.

"Here's how I feel." He began to speak rapidly. "Whatever this town is—Dodge, I mean—we made it. You and me. Look at the dough they take in from tourists—all on account of us. If it hadn't been for us in the old days— what we did—there might not be any Dodge at all—I mean the Texans might have burned it to the ground then, two or three times over. But we saved it, Wyatt—we laid our lives on the line day and night, month in, month out. We brought law and order so the stores and saloons and all could make a hell of a lot of money and the town could

142

grow and—well, look what it is today—thanks to us—
and damn little pay we got for it and damn little thanks."

Wyatt raised the Colt and twirled the cylinder and this
made the sun seem warmer to Bat, even hot, so that he
found a handkerchief and pushed up his hat and gave his
brow a good mop.

"You remember what I said in Grand Central—I said
the West owes us plenty and finally we were gonna collect." Bat began to fan his words like a six-gun. "So that's
what I'm getting at, that's what I'm going round the barn
to say, God I wish you'd put that damn thing away, you're
making me jumpy, now my idea is prob'ly gonna burn
you up, we've been lawmen and stood for law and order
all our lives so breaking the law's the last thing anybody'd
ever expect us to—"

Suddenly, before Bat could move a muscle in reaction,
Wyatt was on his feet and hooking a shoe behind a rear
leg of Bat's chair and pulling and the chair went down on
the planks with a crash and Bat's head with it.

He was dazed.

He blinked.

Wyatt was bent over him.

"Goddamn you, Masterson," he rasped. "When do we
hit the bank?"

"How did you know?"

Wyatt returned the Colt to its holster. "Easy. Two and
two together. We need big money, both of us. Only one
place in Dodge's got that much."

"That's why you used our real names."

"Sure. Who'd believe it? Earp and Masterson back in

Dodge after all these years—much less they'd rob the bank."

"And you're willing?"

"I am. I feel the same way about the West. We're owed. Plenty."

One leaned against one side of an upright under the overhang of the soda-pop Long Branch, one against the other. Bat rubbed the back of his head.

"We better go check out the bank," he said.

"Too late today. Tomorrow. We'll have a lot to do tomorrow. And one thing we get straight now." Wyatt adjusted his slouch hat. "From here on, I call the play."

"You? Who says? It was my idea!"

"I say, city boy. You called it in New York—this is my country. I'm here now."

"What in hell d'you know about robbing a bank?"

Wyatt smiled. "Trust me."

On the way to the hotel they stopped in at the Beeson Museum, paid another 50¢ apiece to a girl at a counter by the door, and idled through three rooms of Indian skulls, skeletons, pottery, warbonnets, bows and arrows, pioneer clothing and cooking utensils, stuffed coyotes, badgers, jackrabbits, beavers, prairie dogs and chickens, eagles, rattlesnakes, cowboy apparel and tools of the cattle trade, rifles, shotguns, handguns until, in the third room, they came face to face with themselves. On a wall was framed a life-sized blowup of a tintype made of them posed together in the '70s. Both were shaved and combed and slicked-up and wore white collarless shirts. Wyatt was seated, Bat stood at his right, and their looks, at the photographer then, at their later, corporeal selves now, were what those of young deputy sheriffs should be—long and level and lawful.

"Why, you scamps," said Wyatt.

"My God I was good-looking!" said Bat.

They were interrupted. A father, mother, son, and daughter wandered into the room and, as Bat and Wyatt moved aside, the tourist family took an interest in the blowup.

"Who's that?" asked the boy.

The father looked below. "Says here, Bat Masterson and Wyatt Earp."

"Who were they?" asked the girl.

"Killers," said her mother.

"How many men'd they shoot?" asked the boy.

"Hundreds."

"Where are they now, Ma?"

"Dead, I expect."

"Serves 'em right," said the girl, and stuck out her tongue at the tintype.

The tourists wandered into another room, but Wyatt had found something else. "See here."

Bat joined him before a glass case in which stood a Sharp's rifle, one huge cartridge on the bottom of the case beside it and a card stuck to the glass: "Wyatt Earp's Buffalo Gun."

"That was my gun. I recollect now. One time I was short in the pocket and Chalk Beeson offered me forty dollars and I sold it—damn him. I paid a hundred for it. Chalk always was tighter than the paper on the wall."

Wyatt looked around. They were alone. Reaching around to the back of the case with a long arm he found a knob and turned it. The back opened. Reaching further, he lifted out the ponderous weapon, then stooping, the cartridge,

145

which he dropped into a pocket, then gave the gun to Bat while he found two twenties in his wallet, placed them on the floor of the case, closed the door, and took the Sharp's.

"There—Chalk's got his forty back. Now you chin with the girl at the door while I get away with this."

Bat was amazed. "What in hell d'you want that old ten-pounder for?"

"Might come in handy."

Bat recollected—in their early Dodge days Wyatt made a practice of hiding shotguns near the doors of stores and saloons up and down Front Street. In an emergency, he said, he wanted something up his sleeve.

"Starting your life of crime early," Bat remarked.

Wyatt held the rifle behind him. "In for a dime, in for a dollar."

A thought made Bat grin. "D'you suppose Chalk's got a big account at the bank?"

They dined that evening at the Popular Cafe on what the menu listed as tenderloin steaks of "Grain-Fed Kansas Beef" and what Bat declared to the waitress was chuck carved off a Texas stray fed on gravel and cactus.

"When I blow a dollar-ten on a steak dinner," he informed her, "I want my money's worth."

"You want me to take it back, sir?"

"To do what with?"

"Well, maybe burn it some more."

"Burial will do. No use cremating it."

"I'm sorry, sir."

"Let me advise you that in the old days around here

you could get a dandy steak dinner at the Delmonico for seventy-five cents."

"Inflation."

The Popular was not very this evening, and by the time the two remaining diners were having at slabs of apple pie they had monopolized both waitresses for coffee refills and conversation.

"What are your names, young ladies?" inquired Mr. Earp.

Mr. Masterson jabbed his tongue with his fork.

"I'm Birdie," said one. "She's Dyjean, my cousin."

"Allow us to introduce ourselves," said Wyatt. "I am Mr. Wyatt Earp. This is Mr. Bat Masterson."

The girls made a face at each other.

Mr. Earp frowned. "Do you doubt my word?"

"Wyatt Earp lives in California," said Dyjean. "And I know for a fact Bat Masterson's a high monkey-monk on a newspaper in New York City."

"So I am," said Bat. "More coffee, please."

"There are trains," reminded Mr. Earp.

"'I Love My Wife But Oh You Kid,'" cracked Birdie, cracking her gum.

"If we had a dollar for every liar who comes in here and claims he's Wyatt Earp or Bat Masterson," said Dyjean, "we wouldn't be slinging hash."

Birdie and Dyjean could not have been called pretty in any context, whether rural or metropolitan, but neither were they homely. The term was "plain." They were big, rawboned girls with big hands and long necks and deep bosoms and wide hips—excellent breeding stock. They were in their late twenties, one would judge, their uniforms were black skirts, ankle length, with white blouses and ticking aprons, and both wore their ordinary brown hair up in buns. There was little to choose between them, except that Birdie was the sparkier, Dyjean the more placid. They called to mind a team of strong, steadfast horses who ploughed a straight furrow and obeyed the bit—a team far more fit for the farm than the fair. They worked hard and slept sound. They had never sampled sugar. Their last name, Mr. Earp ascertained, was Fedder.

"Miss Dyjean," said he, "we're tourists, you might say. Haven't been in Dodge in years. We've seen Old Front Street and the Beeson Museum—now we ought to take in Boot Hill. What time do you young ladies get off work tonight?"

Mr. Masterson swallowed some coffee the wrong way and had to be hit on the back.

"Boot Hill—at night? Oh, gosh, it'd be too scary!" protested Dyjean.

Mr. Earp persisted. "With Wyatt Earp and Bat Masterson to protect you? Surely not. What time?"

"Too late," said Dyjean.

"Too late for you old dears to be up," chirped the saucy Birdie.

"You'd be surprised," continued Mr. Earp. "We old dears can be up whenever we want."

The Fedder cousins flushed and fled into the kitchen, from whence came whoops of laughter.

Mr. Masterson stared at Mr. Earp.

"Why, you old stud!" said Bat.

"I want what I want when I want it," said Wyatt.

They stood outside the Popular Cafe using toothpicks to good effect on the last testaments of Texas steak. Bat was astounded by the change a change of geography had wrought in his friend. Wyatt in New York and Wyatt in Kansas were two different breeds of cat. But then, when he stopped to ponder, while cleaning up his second and third bicuspids, so was he. A New Yorker made, if not born, he was a fish out of water here. Up and down Broadway he had put poor Wyatt through the hoops like a Pomeranian, but that was the Pantages circuit and this was Wyatt's show, so let him run it. Of course, to keep his end up he had to get a word in edgewise now and then.

"Okeh, okeh. But you won't get it from those two," he asserted.

"I won't wear an iron bar for the necktie either. And they'll beat those Ginger bitches all hollow in bed."

"Church girls," scoffed Bat. "About as much in them as a collection box."

"Farmers' daughters," corrected Wyatt. "And we're traveling salesmen."

"We better think about banks, not babes."

"Same thing." Wyatt gave him a man-of-the-world wink. "Deposits first, withdrawals later."

They took in a moving picture at the Bijou because it was too early to retire and also because the feature playing was Bill Hart's latest, "Hell's Hinges," the one he had been in New York to promote the night Runyon and the rest hatched the idea of hiring a gun-thrower to confront Bat in the Knickerbocker Bar.

The theater was small, the seats squeaky, the piano player inept, and the film standard fare. The setting was Hell's Hinges, which, according to the subtitle, was "a good place to ride wide of . . . a gun-fighting, man-killing, devil's den of iniquity." Hart played Blaze Tracey, "the embodiment of the best and the worst of the early West. A man-killer whose philosophy of life is summed up in the creed: shoot first and do your disputin' afterwards." After he met Faith, however, who turned upon him "a different kind of smile, sweet, honest, and trustful," a close-up showed Hart in the grip of doubt: "One who is Evil, looking for the first time on that which is Good." The villain was "Silk Miller: mingling the oily treachery of a Mexican with the deadly craftiness of a rattler, no man's open enemy, and no man's friend." With its leads thus cast in concrete, the plot unreeled. Silk Miller and a mob tried to break up Sunday service officiated over by Faith's brother, a young minister, only to be thwarted by Blaze Tracey, who drew a gun and proclaimed: "I'm announcin' here and now that there ain't goin' to be no more pickin' on the parson's herd." Faith smiled again, creating more conflict in the hero's soul: "I reckon God ain't wantin' me much, Ma'am, but when I look at you I feel I've been ridin' the wrong trail."

Then came considerable footage of men riding hell-bent across deserts and over mountains, during which the piano player, who should have been doing "The Light Cavalry Overture," rendered "The Road to Mandalay"—a glaring error accounted for either by ennui or ignorance of his art. Matters came to a climax, conventionally enough, in a saloon. Silk Miller murdered the minister. Faith wept buckets over the body. Hart arrived on his stalwart stallion "Fritz," kicked open the doors, and over drawn guns shouted, "Hell needs this town, and it's goin' back, and goin' damn quick!" With a passion almost pyromaniacal, he then proceeded to gun Miller and several of his henchmen down, to ignite the saloon by shooting out the kerosene lamps, to save Faith, allow the "soiled doves" to escape, and finally to see to it that the entire degenerate town went up in flames.

At the height of the conflagration, Wyatt nudged Bat and muttered "Let's go." They headed for a side exit, and Bat was about to open the door when, to his flabbergastment, Wyatt pulled his pistol, aimed, and fired a round right through the sheet music on the instrument in front of the piano player. This made for a big night at the Bijou. There were shouts and screams, and patrons tried to do headers under seats, and the piano player streaked off his stool like a rocket and leaped on stage and ran across the screen, and Bat and Wyatt took a powder outside to stroll down the street as though out for an evening's constitutional.

"What in hell did you do that for!" demanded Bat.

"The piano player," said Wyatt, cool as lemonade made in the shade. "He wasn't doing the best he could."

"Well, my God!"

Wyatt stretched himself. "Got a crick in my neck. Also, he reminded me of Al, at the Belasco—you remember him. Wanted my autograph."

"Wyatt, I don't know what's got into you."

"Also, I never saw such a pile of sheepshit. I was proud to meet Hart back east, but he should be ashamed of himself."

They strolled a block in silence.

"They really roll up the sidewalks in Dodge now, don't they?" commented Bat. "No action anywhere—you can't even get a drink. Hell, the old days this town never closed."

"How about if we see the girls are off work yet?"

"You don't mean it."

"I beg to differ."

"But it's late!"

"Can't be ten o'clock yet."

151

"Well, I'm whipped."

"You? The night-lifer? Why, you never fold before five in the morning."

"You're not funny. I need to hit the hay—must be the fresh air out here."

They neared the O'Neal House.

"Maybe you're getting too old," Wyatt mused.

"To what?"

"Hear the wolf howl."

Next morning, that of the 4th May, at three minutes of ten, they stood across the street from the Drovers Bank of Dodge City. It was an imposing two-story structure, built of white glazed brick with glazed Grecian columns on either side of the doors, which opened, evidently, at ten. Two women waited at them, and a man.

"Pretty fancy for a hick bank," said Bat.

"Um."

"Just sitting there waiting to be taken. Easy as shuckin' corn."

"Um."

"Wonder how much cash they keep on hand. D'you suppose as much as fifty, sixty thousand?"

Wyatt shrugged. "They might. Town's ten times as big as it was then. And all that wheat money."

"Why don't I ask?"

Wyatt looked at him. "Sometimes I think you'll never carry a full string of fish. No, just go to a teller and change some bills. Meantime, I'll get the layout of the place."

"Have you got a plan yet?"

"I'll think of something."

The doors were unlocked, and the man and two women admitted.

"Off to the races," said Bat, cocking his derby.

To the left were three tellers' windows.

Bat went to one of them.

Wyatt leaned an elbow on one of the high customers' tables centered down the marble floor.

The interior of the Drovers Bank was as plush as the ex. To the right, as you entered, behind a low oaken rail, a carpeted open area ran the length of the bank. Here were desks for clerks and minor officers. Behind these, in the center, was the open door to the vault.

Bat was talking to a lady teller who, unfortunately, happened to be young and, even more unfortunately, as far as Wyatt was concerned, a looker.

He could locate only one enclosed office, to his immediate right, on the street end, with a plaque on the door. After a couple of squints he made out what he thought was "Wm. J. Beanstone, President & Cashier."

Bat talked to the looker.

Hung on the walls in great gilt frames were oil paintings of subjects indigenous to and symbolic of Kansas—grain elevators and barns and farm machinery such as reapers and threshers and cornhuskers and manure spreaders.

The looker talked to Bat.

Search as he might, Wyatt could find only one back door, to the right, in the rear of the open office area.

Bat and the looker talked to each other.

Wyatt rearranged some splayed hairs in his mustache. Then he drummed on the customer table with fingertips.

153

Then he bit a lip. When it was all he could manage to resist going to Bat and grabbing him by the collar, he walked out of the bank and took up position across the street.

Bat strutted across the street humming, "The Darktown Strutters Ball."

"Say, did you see the dolly I was talking to? What a looker!"

"Damn you—I told you to change some bills and get out! What in hell were you up to?"

"Talking, is all. I said we're new in town and might be depositors and what was she doing tonight?"

Wyatt bit the other lip and blew some air. "Well, it should be a cinch. There's one back door in plain sight, the vault's in the center."

"Her name's Millie Sughrue—her father-in-law's the sheriff."

"The sheriff!"

"So she's married. I told her that's no problem, so am I."

"Now listen. Two men can do it. One minute after the doors are unlocked, like this morning, we go in, masked. We get the tellers and any customers down on the floor. The others stay at their desks, hands up—they have guns in those desks sometimes. One of us goes in with the tellers and cleans out the cash drawers while the other covers everybody. Then the first one covers while the other takes an officer into the vault. We'll use their money bags— they've always got bags lying around."

"She gave me a ruler."

"What we'll have to watch is the president—he's in an

office in the front. He could telephone the law or set off an alarm or open a window and yell—one of us better go in right away and bring him out and put him on the floor. Name on the door's Beanstone."

"They give rulers to everybody, she said, to encourage thrift. I said I was hot for thrift." Bat held it up to display the maxim in large black letters: "A Penny Saved Is A Penny Earned." "Nice, huh?"

"Any more customers come in while we're working, they hit the floor, too. I'd say, if we work easy and steady, we should be out of there in five minutes."

"Where do we hold the horses?"

Wyatt looked at him.

"Where do we hold the horses?" Bat repeated.

Wyatt looked at him as one looks at a child. "Horses, Bat? Horses?"

"Horses."

Wyatt took him gently by both shoulders. "You've been taking in too many Western movies. Either that or you're going dotty. Now listen to me, Bat. How many years since you've been up on a horse?"

"Well, that's—"

"You'd fall off."

"I don't think—"

"Bat, this is 1916."

"Oh."

"There's more automobiles on the road than horses now. We'll use an automobile."

"Oh. How about a taxi?"

"No. This isn't New York."

"Oh. Can you drive a car?"

"No. But you can."

"Me?"

"Yes, you, Barney Oldfield."

155

Coat off, shirtsleeves rolled up, hat hung over the Moto-Meter, Mr. Masterson cranked and cranked and cranked. When the engine caught, he raced around to reach under the steering wheel to move the spark and throttle levers from starting position to idle—but not in time. The engine died. This was his third exercise in futility. Puffing, face red with rage, he pounded a fist on the doortop.

"Goddamn this thing to hell!"

Mr. Earp lounged on the passenger side of the seat, one foot up at ease on the dashboard. "How can we make a getaway tomorrow morning," he inquired reasonably enough, "if you can't even start the car?"

They had gone directly from the bank to the Dodge City Livery and hired a Ford Model T Touring Sedan—two dollars a day, cash money, two days or four dollars in advance as a deposit, and the proprietor had given Mr. Masterson rudimentary instruction in starting and operating the vehicle free of charge. It started for him at once, and ran. Parked behind the livery garage, it would start for Mr. Masterson, but refused to run.

"Maybe you're not getting around here from the front end fast enough," theorized Mr. Earp. "Not as spry as you used to be."

Mr. Masterson glared. "Why do I have to do the leg work?"

"I plan the job, you handle the car. And collect rulers."

"Why do we have to hire this sardine can? Why can't we show some class? How about a Chandler? Or a Hudson Super-Six?"

"More T's on the road than anything else. One more

won't be noticed." Mr. Earp pointed at a pile of empty quart oilcans. "Pitch me a couple of those, will you?"

Mr. Masterson stepped to the pile, picked up two cans, toed the rubber, wound up, and one after another hurled them at him with the control and velocity of a Grover Cleveland Alexander. Mr. Earp gloved one neatly in each hand and dropped them on the floor of the rear seat compartment.

"If at first you don't succeed," he hinted.

Again Mr. Masterson bent to his toil and whirled the crank. Again the engine came to life and the chauffeur raced around the hood to the levers under the steering wheel. This time the twenty horses under the hood calmed down to a contented canter.

A sneer of success about his lips, Mr. Masterson rolled down his sleeves, donned his coat, retrieved his hat, and eased into the driver's seat.

As he understood it, there were three pedals in the floorboard under the wheel—clutch to the left, reverse in the center, and brake on the right—or was it the other way round? And there were nine lever settings on the notched quadrant on the steering post—spark to the left, throttle to the right—or was it the opposite?

He pushed the clutch pedal halfway down, which was neutral, advanced spark and throttle levers a couple of notches, pushed the clutch to the floor, simultaneously and confidently hit one of the other pedals, and with a grind of gears and a crunch of metal bucked them backward into the brick wall of the garage.

"Hey, hey! How'm I doin'?"

His passenger did not respond.

Ooooo-gah! Ooooo-gah! Bat banged the hand-operated brass-belled Klaxon horn.

His passenger did not respond.

"I love it! I could ride this flivver till the cows come home!"

His passenger did not respond. Hands gripping the top of the windshield, Wyatt sat rigid on the edge of the seat as though the Twentieth Century were a muzzle and he was staring into it.

They chugged along at ten mph, according to the Stewart speedometer attached to the dashboard, on a narrow macadam road headed east out of Dodge. Instead of a cap, the radiator was crowned by the latest accessory—a winged brass Boyce Moto-Meter, faced with glass and inset with a red-level temperature gauge scaled from "Good Average" to "High Efficiency" to "Danger—Steaming!" The red line stood at "Good Average." With the top of the touring sedan down, the morning breeze was fresh in their faces. A sign informed them that four miles down the road lay the village of Garden of Eden, but without the grain elevator which stuck out above the flatland like a sore thumb, they would never have known there was a village. Habitations and inhabitants were hidden in trees.

"Stop!" shouted Wyatt.

"Why?"

"Stop!"

Bat found the clutch and brake and stopped. Wyatt opened his door, dismounted, closed the door, looked up and down the road. Except for a wagon a mile or more away, it was clear. Wyatt stepped clear of the car.

"All right, let's see you back 'er up."

"I don't know how."

"I know that. But there's nothing out here for you to back into. You better know how."

"Why?"

"In case you need to tomorrow."

"Oh." Bat changed the subject. "Speaking of that— whatta we do after the bank? We can't sit in the car on Front Street and count the loot. I s'pose you've got that planned, too."

"I have. We'll drive out this way as far as that town—" Wyatt pointed down the road at Garden of Eden— "then turn north a couple of miles, then drive west a few miles, then south to this road, then come into Dodge again from the west. Sort of a big square. Then right down Front Street to the hotel as though we've just been out for a spin."

"Now who's dotty?"

"Not me. Who'd ever believe it? That anybody'd rob a bank and get away and drive right back into town, big as life? Same principle as our names. Nobody believes those either."

"Okeh, then what?"

"Simple. We hang around Dodge the rest of the day as though nothing's happened. Tomorrow night we have supper at the Popular, say goodbye to the girls, split the cash, and get a good night's sleep. Next morning we go to the station and wait for our trains and kiss goodbye. You go your way, I go mine."

Bat was dubious. "I dunno. Sounds too easy."

"That's the beauty of it. Anyway, quit talking me in circles. Let's see you back this contraption up."

"I said I can't."

"I say you can."

"I'm not sure which pedal. This damn thing really takes three legs."

"Go ahead, try it."

"Goddammit, no. Bat Masterson and Wyatt Earp never back up!"

"No guts."

That did it. Bat shoved at the spark and throttle levers and jammed at least two pedals and the Tin Lizzie roared and bucked and began to back down the road faster and faster yet.

"Whoa!" cried Bat. "Whoa!"

But it was only after jerking levers and playing the pedals like those of an organ that he stopped the car eventually, at the same time stalling the engine.

An expressionless Wyatt walked to the automobile, slid into the passenger seat, closed the door, and propped a foot up at ease on the dashboard.

"Get cranking," he said.

Bat set his jaw. "Go to hell."

"No ambition."

"You crank!"

His friend considered, then said, "Let me remind you. The last night in New York you said it was time to pick our peaches—and you knew how. How to get rich. You'd just had the most sensational son-of-a-bitch idea you ever had in your whole life."

Bat considered, then set the levers, got out, hung his derby on the Moto-Meter, and began to crank.

After another half-mile of motoring, Wyatt directed his driver to slow down and turn off and stop before a gate in a fence. He got out, opened the gate, waved the driver through, told him to cut the engine, then took the two empty quart oilcans from the rear seat compartment and set them atop two fenceposts.

"How long since you fired a gun?" he asked. "I'm not talking about blanks."

"Oh my God," admitted Bat.

"Likewise."

Bat got out of the Ford and they paced off approximately twenty yards from the posts and took places and unbuttoned jackets.

In his article on Wyatt Earp in *Human Life*, Bat had stated flatly that "Wyatt's speed and skill with a six-gun made almost any play against him with weapons 'no contest.' Possibly there were more accomplished trick-shots than he, but in all my years in the West at its wildest, I never saw the man in action who could shade him in the prime essential of real gun-fighting—the draw-and-shoot against something that could shoot back. In a day when almost every man possessed as a matter of course the ability to get a six-gun into action with a rapidity that a later generation simply will not credit, Wyatt's speed...was considered phenomenal by those who literally were marvels at the same feat. His marksmanship at any range from four to four hundred yards was a perfect complement to his speed. On more than one occasion I have seen him kill coyotes at the latter distance with his Colt's, and any man who has ever handled a six-gun will tell you that, while luck figures largely in such shooting, only a past-master of the weapon could do that."

Wyatt's right hand swept under his jacket toward his left shoulder. He drew, and as his gun-hand dropped, he fired at the oilcan sixty feet before him on the fencepost and missed.

Bat made no remark. He believed, and had been so quoted, that the three qualities a man needed to rank as an expert with a revolver were courage, skill at handling his weapon, and, not least, the ability and coolness to make the first shot count. He had been even more specific, writing once that "A lot of inexperienced fellows try to aim a six-shooter by sighting along the barrel, and they try to shoot the other man in the head. Never do that. If you have to stop a man with a gun, grab the stock of your six-shooter with a death-grip that won't let it wobble, and try to hit him just where the belt buckle would be. That's the broadest target from head to heel. If you point at something, you don't raise your finger to a level of the eye and sight along it; you simply point, by instinct, and your finger will always point straight. So you must learn to point the barrel of your six-shooter by instinct. If you haven't that direction instinct born in you, you will never become an expert with the six-gun."

Bat's right hand swept under his jacket toward his left shoulder. He drew, and as his gun-hand dropped, he fired at the oilcan sixty feet before him on the fencepost and missed.

Wyatt made no remark. He said only, after he had replaced his weapon, "Let's get to it."

They drew together, and fired again together, and missed.

"It's these damn shoulder holsters," said Wyatt after a moment.

"You're right."

"I'm used to hardware on my hip."

"So'm I."

"And shooting from there."

"Me, too," Bat agreed. "Tell you what—the hell with the holsters. Let our guns hang down and pretend we're drawing. Just like the old days, only no holster at all."

They positioned themselves, and this time let the old Colts hang at their sides, then suddenly raised them and fired at the two oilcans and missed.

Each examined his six-gun in silence.

"I've had enough," said Bat.

"Likewise." Wyatt took a box of bullets from a coat pocket. "Let's not forget to reload—we did that once."

They reloaded in silence.

"Right shoulder bothers me when I raise my arm," said Wyatt. "I told you—arthritis."

"Emma's been after me about glasses," said Bat. "Nearsighted."

They put pistols away.

"Oh, well," said Bat. "We don't want to shoot anybody anyway, do we?"

They meandered back to the automobile. Bat climbed behind the wheel, but instead of mounting up, Wyatt sat down on the grass in front of the car.

"Bat, I've been thinking. You recollect what Mr. Roosevelt said about us?"

"What?"

"You know—that we'll be legends or something someday. They'll write a lot of books about us. He said if we're

famous now, just wait'll we're dead and gone. Tell me—
you think it's true?"

Bat got out of the car, came round to the front end, and
with a grunt sat down beside him. "Why not? I'd say we're
damn good material."

Wyatt reflected. "Well, so far so good. But we've got to
do this job right tomorrow. We can't throw any lead and
we've got to get away clean. If we're caught, we lose everything—and I don't mean just the money. Our names'll be
mud."

"I'll go along with that."

Bat lit up a Spud. Wyatt lit up a cigar. He'd been pleased
to find one thing in Dodge unchanged: a good Mexican
Commerce cigar was still 5¢. He took off his hat and laid
his head back against the acetylene-gas headlamp. Bat took
his off and used the other lamp.

"You feeling squeamish about tomorrow?" he asked.

"Some."

"Why? We're owed."

"Even so, we've never been on the off side of the law
before."

"You scared?"

"I wish my shoulder was better. And my knee. And
your eyesight. And we were ten years younger."

Bat tried a smoke ring. "'Where do we hold the horses?'
Talk about a dumb thing to say. It's just hard for me to
get used to so much change all the time. Why, Dodge is
so different I don't even recognize it. And look at this."

He gestured at what lay before them. They sat on grass
by the fence on one side of a pasture. As far as the eye
could see—which seemed at least as far as the LaSalle
Station in Chicago—fields of spring wheat succeeded fields
of short corn, all fenced and neat and fertilized and trac-
tored and farmered. Where, every half-mile, a clump of

trees flawed country that had once been bare as a billiard ball, there was a farmhouse, and where, every three or four miles, a grain elevator towered, there was a village tucked away in more trees like Garden of Eden. Forty years before, this had been pristine prairie. Buffalo in their millions had fed and fought and dropped calves and wallowed. Cheyenne and Comanche in their thousands had fed and fought and reproduced and danced. Wagon trains of pilgrims in their hundreds had fed and fought and found, at the end of the trail, freedom. And now look at it.

This they did. And the longer they looked, the more clearly they saw. It was what a day in May was designed to be. The land was as illimitable as ever, the blue sky as boundless. There were long low rises, and folds between, and the fields were green as ever the lonesome prairie once had been. The trees, planted as breaks against the scything winds of winter, were tamaracks and cottonwoods and Chinese elms and sycamores. The song of meadowlarks in the sky was lovely. And the longer they looked at what was once called "Bloody Kansas," the more clearly they saw what this new and husbanded place could be at peace. If Kansas had been beautiful then, when they were young, it was beautiful still, the way their hearts were youthful still, and would be till they beat no more.

"All that wheat," said Bat, embarrassed by sentiment. "Breadbasket of the world."

"Yup."

Then Bat said what he really wanted to say. "By God, Wyatt, it's still beautiful. God's country."

"It is that."

"I'd forgotten. New York's swell, but this is—well, special. I wouldn't even mind being planted out here someday, would you?"

"Nope."

Bat stubbed his Spud in the grass. "Most of us guna-rounds already gone, you know. Luke Short, Charlie B., old Mysterious Dave."

"Doc. Ben Thompson. Clay."

"The James boys, all the Daltons but one."

"Hickok. Hardin. Doolin."

"That's a hell of a long list, Wyatt."

"J.B. Books, too. You hear what he did?"

"No."

"Well, he was down in El Paso. Had a cancer, and but a few weeks left," Wyatt related. "So he sent word to three of four of the hard cases around to show up in a saloon and he'd be there with his guns on. They did and Books was. Killed 'em all, by God, and got put out of his misery himself. Cleaned up the whole town."

"I'll be damned. A great way to go—do some good while you're at it."

"And my brother Morg. That's about the worst thing ever happened to me, Bat."

"I know. Like my brother Ed. I can still get blue about that. How're your other brothers?"

"Jim's all right. Virg went ten years ago—natural causes. What about the Mastersons?"

"Tom's still on the farm. Jim and George both dead."

"Sorry to hear that."

"Anyway," Bat said, "we must be about the last with our boots on. Us and Bill Tilghman. Makes you think."

"Sure does."

They thought for a while.

"Fifty, sixty thousand in that bank—that's what you figured," said Bat presently. "Twenty, thirty, apiece. What'll you do with yours?"

"Stop being a squaw man." Wyatt drew deeply on the Mexican Commerce. "I mean, Josie gives me money when

I ask for it, but I hate like sin to. I'll pay her back every penny."

"I'll pay Grogan off first thing I get home. Waltz in there and throw down the cash—damn his socks. Then see about some life insurance—never believed in it. You have any? Life insurance?"

Bat looked over. Wyatt was taking a cat nap, cigar burning between his fingers. He had an idea. Carefully he got up off the grass, carefully sneaked around the T to the Klaxon horn near the steering wheel, placed a palm over the plunger, and rammed it down.

Ooooo-gah!

"Ya-hoooo!"

Bat whooped and waved his derby as though he were breaking a bronc and riding high. He'd shoved the spark and throttle levers up to full-speed position, and the Touring Sedan yipped along the road toward Dodge like a mutt with a tin can tied to its tail. Hat jammed down to his eyes, Wyatt clung to the windshield like a drowning man to a straw. They passed a Diamond T truck as though it were standing still. Then over the clamor of the car they heard the siren, and who should roar alongside but Peace Officer Harvey Wadsworth, who waved them down and, when Bat had pulled off, parked his Indian Powerplus up ahead and walked back to them with pride in his stride.

"Good day, gents. Well, well, if it isn't our great gunfighters. Where were you going—to a fire?"

"Just seeing what this crowbait would do if I put the spur to 'er," smiled Bat.

The P.O. shook his head. "You old boys are hell on

wheels, all right." He took pad and pencil from a pocket and began to write. "You were doing forty—I clocked you—and thirty-five is as high as she goes in Kansas. Gonna have to give you a ticket."

"To what?" Bat inquired. "The Policeman's Ball?"

"To an appearance before the town magistrate. Speeding. It'll cost you ten dollars."

"Ten dollars!" exclaimed Bat. "How in hell am I supposed to know the speed limit in Kansas?"

"Ignorance of the law is no excuse," said Wyatt, butting in and raising his hat.

"You know who we are!" Bat appealed. "How can Dodge City charge Bat Masterson?"

Harvey Wadsworth stayed his pencil.

"An ex-marshal breaks the law, that's the lowest," said Wyatt. "Book 'im."

"Goddammit, Wyatt, shut up!" cried Bat. He pulled an importunate face. "What if we don't have the funds?"

The P.O. beamed and twinkled as he tore off the ticket. "Pass the hat. Who wouldn't help Wyatt Earp and Bat Masterson around here? I'd ante up a dime myself."

Bat folded the ticket. "Well, hell, all right. I'll get my ten bucks back from the town one way or another. Tell me, d'you pass out many of these?"

"How d'you think they pay my salary?" The long arm of the local law sobered up and saluted. "Good day, gents. And take it easy."

"Yes, sir, Ossifer," said Bat. "I'll tie 'er down to a trot."

They moseyed into the Long Branch Pharmacy on Front Street. Two big glass globes hung from the ceiling down over the counter, both containing liquid, evidently, one blue and one orange. Before the turn of the century, these had been used as retorts in which to percolate herbs and medicinal substances—peppermint leaves and alcohol, for example, produced peppermint oil; digitalis leaves and other chemicals, digitalis for heart patients. Now they survived as eye-catchers.

"Something I can do for you?" asked the pharmacist in white jacket and long nose and rimless specs.

"I want to buy some whiskey," announced Wyatt. "Two pints—easy to carry."

"Medicinal purposes?" asked the pharmacist.

"You could say so."

"I sure need it," added Bat. "Just got a speeding ticket."

"Harvey nabbed another one, huh?"

Bat winked. "Also we've got a date tonight. Our age, you need a tonic."

The pharmacist turned solemn. "Well, we're dry, you know. Got a doctor's prescription? Can't wet your whistle without a prescription."

"I have one," said Wyatt. "From Dr. Colt."

"Hmmm, Dr. Colt...Dr. Colt..." The pharmacist frowned. "Can't rightly say I know a Dr. Colt."

Wyatt moved round the end of the counter to him, drew three pounds of steel from under his jacket, and placed the muzzle in the pharmacist's ear.

"You know him now," said he.

"Yessir, I sure do, sir." The pharmacist selected two pint bottles from a goodly stock under the counter, and placing one under the spigot at the side of the blue globe, began to fill.

"Blue whiskey?" said Bat.

"Yes, sir," replied the pharmacist. "Blue whiskey, and orange gin in the other one. That's how I keep it—state

169

liquor agents in and out of here all the time."

"Looks like embalming fluid," Bat commented. "D'you turn blue when you drink it?"

"Not a bit," the pharmacist assured him. "Leastwise my best customer says not."

"Who's that?"

"The undertaker."

The lights went out in the Popular Cafe that night at ten o'clock. Like drugstore cowboys champing at the bit, Bat and Wyatt waited on the sidewalk in front for the Fedder fillies.

"They'll be out any minute," said Wyatt. "You take Birdie—she's more your type. I'll handle good ol' Dyjean."

"It isn't gonna work," worried Bat.

"With blue whiskey it will."

"They think we're too old."

"They'll be surprised."

"They said so, last night."

"You wait."

"You know how much luck we had with those damn Ginger Sisters."

"We're home. Our luck's changed."

"They don't even believe who we are—we don't have a prayer."

"You wait," declared Wyatt. "Listen, even a blind sow picks up an acorn now and then."

Arms entwined, a few paces apart, two couples strolled past the Beeson Museum and Old Front Street toward Boot Hill. The stars were fat, the moon was skinny. The night was a retort in which various elements percolated, so that the air was aromatic of growing grain and broken dreams and bank vaults and oil of romance and cattle pens and sexual satisfaction or your money back.

"You got the gift of gab, all right, whoever you are," admitted Birdie Fedder.

"Whoever I am?" said Bat. "I assure you, my dear, that I am W.B. Masterson, a sports writer for the New York *Morning Telegraph*—my column's in it every day."

"I'll catch you yet. Kids growing up around here learn a lot about Masterson and Earp."

"They do? Glad to hear it."

"If you're actually Wyatt Earp," said Dyjean Fedder, "what're you doing back in Dodge?"

"I'm sorry," said Wyatt, "but I can't say."

"I thought not. You're just handing me a line. We know a lot about Earp and Masterson around here."

"Is that a fact."

The young ladies wore their waitress uniforms, but they had taken off the ticking aprons.

"You've never been to New York, I presume?" Bat inquired of Birdie.

"Are you kidding? I went to Wichita once, though. Do they really have trains that run under the ground?"

"Subways? They certainly do. A nickel a ride—from the Bronx into Manhattan and on to Brooklyn."

"You could of read all that in a book."

"Could have but didn't. I happen to have some liquid refreshment with me," Bat purred, producing the pint. "Would you care for a nip, my dear?"

"Don't mind if I do."

Birdie uncorked the bottle and fired down a dram. Bat followed her example. She was taller than he, and already rising in his esteem.

"I know Wyatt Earp lives in California," said Dyjean.

"He does. I do."

"Where?"

"Well, I've lived in San Diego and spent considerable time in San Francisco, and I have a house now in Vidal. Have you been to California?"

"Don't make me laugh. Garden City, Kansas—fifty-three miles. That's how far west I been."

"And east?"

"Wichita. Me and Birdie went once."

"I have some whiskey." Wyatt produced a pint. "Like a drink?"

"Sure, why not?"

Dyjean uncorked the bottle and give it a good tilt, a sociable act which seemed to Wyatt, as he followed her example, a hopeful sign.

"You're married," Birdie accused Bat as they resumed their stroll.

"That's right. Twice over."

"Twice!"

"I have two Indian wives. Comanche. Took 'em with me to New York and put 'em in vaudeville. They've got a crackerjack act—shoot arrows at each other and throw tommyhawks and bring me in a damn good income."

Birdie giggled. "You liar. You've got one wife and you're

a real live wire. You all are. I bet you give your old lady fits."

"I bet I do. But listen, she's no duck soup to live with either."

"How long've you been hitched?"

"Twenty-five years."

"No kidding. Say, how old are you?"

"Old enough to know better."

"I'll drink to that."

Birdie stopped and held out a hand. A gracious Bat gladly produced the bottle.

"Are you married?" Dyjean asked Wyatt.

"I am."

"Well, that's something."

"What?"

"That you'd say so. They never do. They always say they're not till they get what they want and then they tell you they are. Married. I wish I was."

"You should be. A strapping girl like you'd make someone a mighty fine wife."

"Don't say that."

"What's wrong?"

"I might cry."

"Here." Wyatt stopped and quickly produced the pint. "This will help."

Dyjean uncorked. "Thank you."

"You're welcome."

"You're nice, whoever you are."

"Thank you, Dyjean."

Two steps and two snorts later they reached Boot Hill and gathered in a foursome to take in the sight. What they saw was a puny, pee-poor grassed area with a gravel walkway through it and surrounded by a low stone wall. A number of headboards were stuck here and there, the lumber suspiciously new, with burnt-in names and dates and epitaphs: Levi Richardson, Cockeyed Frank, Dora Hand, Alkali Ike, Toothless Nell, Two-Toed Pete, etc.

"Damnation," said Bat in disgust. "This isn't Boot Hill."

"Another damn tourist trap," said Wyatt.

"How would you two know?" asked Dyjean.

"How would we know?" demanded Bat. "Because we did a hell of a lot of planting up here, that's why! And because I recollect they dug 'em all up and moved 'em out to Prairie Grove Cemetery—when was that, Wyatt?"

"Around '79."

"I thought maybe they'd brought some of 'em back, but they haven't," said Bat, subsiding. "Just another damn game for the ginks, that's all."

"Well, ha-ha-ha, this takes the cake," jibed Birdie, hands on hips. "A fake Bat Masterson and a fake Wyatt Earp come back to a fake Boot Hill."

The two males scowled at her.

"Come on, don't go 'way mad," she said, slipping her arm in Bat's.

"No, don't get all het up," said Dyjean, slipping her arm in Wyatt's.

"Okeh," said Bat.

"Likewise," said Wyatt.

They strolled the gravel walkway through the headboards, then separated, each couple sitting in the starlight at a discreet distance from the other on the low stone wall, each gentleman's arm about his lady's waist as they studied the names and dates and epitaphs and partook of Dr. Colt's prescription from the Long Branch Pharmacy and whispered sweet nothings in the nearest ear.

EDWARD HURLEY

SHOT JAN. 1873
HE DRANK TOO
MUCH AND LOVED
UNWISELY

"Where you from, Birdie girl?" Bat inquired.
"Right here—where else?" she sighed.
"Dodge?"
"No such luck. Down on the farm—Ford County. Six-
teen miles south of here. You hiding the bottle?"
"No, here."
Birdie had one for Ford County.
"Big family?"
"Three brothers and three sisters—I was the middle girl.
Fat chance I had."
"So you came up to Dodge."
"I was twenty-one."
"The bright lights."
"I could see my future on the farm—there wasn't none.
An old maid for sure."
"Stuck in the kitchen."
"And no tips."

GEORGE HOYT

SHOT JULY 26,
1878 ONE NIGHT
HE TOOK A
POTSHOT AT WYATT
EARP "LET HIS
FAULTS, IF ANY,
BE HIDDEN IN
THE GRAVE"

175

"Me and Birdie are cousins—her folks' farm was just down the road from ours."

"Sodders?" Wyatt asked.

"Our grandfolks. Sod houses and all that, way back when. I guess they had it awful hard."

"They sure did. How come you came to Dodge?"

"Well, we was both in the same boat. Cook and do chores and hope some boy with cowshit on his shoes would marry us so we could cook and do chores. Our folks didn't mind we left—one less mouth to feed. So we come to Dodge and took a room together and waited for the lightning to strike. Been here seven years now."

"How's it turned out?"

Dyjean hesitated. "I can't even talk about it 'less I have a drink."

"Certainly."

Dyjean hung the bottle high and long.

"Blue," said she, wiping her lips with the back of her hand. "Long Branch."

SHOOT-EM-UP JAKE
RUN FOR SHERIFF
1872 RUN FROM
SHERIFF 1876
BURIED 1876

"Anyways," Birdie continued, "we roomed together and got waitress jobs at the Popular and been there ever since. Waitressing, waiting—same difference."

"For what?"

"Whatta you think?"

This time Birdie didn't ask for the bottle. She took it. But before she could drain it, Bat grabbed it back. This girl had a hollow leg.

"We was young and dumb," she said. "We thought we'd have lots of dates and we could pick and choose— oh, brother. The town boys wouldn't give us the time of day—they go with the town girls. George Beanstone and those stuck-up bastards."

"Beanstone?"

"The banker's son. Anyways, we soon found out, me and Dyjean. If we wanted any fun, we had to take it where we could get it."

"Where was that?"

"The O'Neal House."

"The O'Neal House?"

"Where we'll be in about ten minutes after you get us boozed up enough."

"Why, we wouldn't—"

"The hell you wouldn't!" Birdie suddenly dissolved. "Traveling salesmen!" she blubbered, hitting him in the chest with a fist. "Old coots like you!"

JACK WAGNER

KILLED ED
MASTERSON
APRIL 19,
1878 HE AR-
GUED WITH
THE WRONG
MAN'S BROTHER

"It didn't," said Dyjean. "Turn out, I mean. We been at the Popular seven years. I was twenty-one when Birdie and me come to Dodge—do your own 'rithmetic. The town boys couldn't see us for sour apples."

"That's too bad."

"Too bad? That's terrible! How many library books can you read? How many picture shows can you go to on your nights off? How lonesome can a body be?"

Before Wyatt could offer consolation, Dyjean had the bottle and provided her own. He polished off the little left. This girl had a hollow leg.

"You must have a little fun now and then," he said lamely. "Everybody does."

"Oh sure."

To his embarrassment, Dyjean suddenly burst into tears and buried her face in his chest.

"Oh sure we do! Just like tonight!"

"Tonight?"

"Drinking and sitting around looking at old graves and then going to the hotel!"

"The hotel? We wouldn't—"

"The hell you wouldn't!" Dyjean bawled into his shirt front. "We're whores now, me'n Birdie—no better'n whores! Only we don't get paid for it—all's we get's blue-boo-hoo whiskey!"

ALICE CHAMBERS

DIED 1878 SHE
WAS A FAVORITE
OF MANY "CIR-
CUMSTANCES LED
ME TO THIS END"

"We don't need a light," whispered Birdie.

"Okeh," whispered Bat.

"Where's him and Dyjean?"

"Next room. 110."

"Could they walk in on us?"

"Door between's locked."

"Is there a key?"

"No."

Birdie took off her blouse and skirt. Bat took off his coat and slung it over the back of a chair.

"What in the world's that?"

"A shoulder holster."

"No, I mean in it."

He took it out. "My gun."

"I've never seen such a big gun—yes I have. In the Beeson Museum. What is it?"

"A Colt forty-five."

"That's what they used in those days, wasn't it? Bat Masterson and Wyatt Earp."

"We still do."

Birdie sat down on the side of the bed and stared at him as he put the gun away and took off holster and tie and shirt.

"My God," she whispered.

"My God what?"

"What if you really are Bat Masterson?"

"No light," whispered Dyjean.

"Fine with me," whispered Wyatt.

"Where are they?"

"Next room. 112."

"Might they walk in on us through that door?"

"It's locked."

"What about a key?"

"None I know of."

Dyjean took off her blouse and skirt. Wyatt took off his

coat and hung it carefully in the closet.

"Why, that must be from the Civil War!"

"What?"

"That gun! Let's see it."

He took it out.

"Goodness gracious."

"I told you who I am."

Dyjean sat down on the side of the bed and stared at him as he put the gun away and took off holster and tie and shirt.

"Wyatt Earp," she whispered.

"Now do you believe me?"

"Just about."

Birdie unbuttoned her high-button shoes and unrolled her hose. Bat grunted out of his shoes, slung his trousers on top of his coat, and divested himself of his BVD's. Birdie stood, dropped her bloomers, and unhooked her corset.

"How come you leave on your socks?" she whispered.

"Feet get cold nights," he whispered.

"Oh."

Bat piled into bed and sank practically out of sight. "I haven't slept on a feather tick since I was a pup."

"They've put mattresses in most rooms, but I guess they haven't got around to this one yet."

Birdie unhooked a massive cotton brassiere and hung it over a bedpost.

"What a pair!" complimented Bat.

"Thanks."

He slid over and plumped up a pillow for her. "Come on in, Buttercup—the water's fine."

180

"I will in a minute." Birdie sat down on the edge of the bed beside him in the buff. "You've about made a believer out of me—that gun and how much you know about Boot Hill and all. Just one more thing, Mister. I like to know who I'm sleeping with. I'm gonna give you a quiz. Who was Molly Brennan?"

"Oh my God," groaned Bat. "That's a long story—I can't wait!"

"You'll have to," said an adamant Birdie, stretching out sideways and hanging her pair over him like Golden Delicious on a big warm bough. "I know who she was and what happened. Let's see if you do."

After some debate Bat began, rushing his narrative and skipping some of the more sordid details. In the summer of '75, when he was a young buck of twenty-one, just after he'd scouted the Staked Plains for Colonel Miles and assisted in the rescue of the Germain sisters from Stone Calf's band of Cheyenne, he'd been resting up between adventures in Sweetwater, Texas. There he'd fallen in love with a blue-eyed, black-haired beauty named Molly Brennan, a saloon girl with a heart of silver who fell, fortunately, like a ton of bricks for him. Her boss, the saloon keeper, had given them a key to the place so they could cavort in the vineyards of love after hours, and this they did to their mutual benefit. Molly had, unfortunately, another flame, the infamous Sergeant King of the Fourth Cavalry, a brawler and a gunner and with the ladies as slippery as a greased pig. He was in a vile mood that summer to boot. Earlier on, in Wichita, he had dared to draw on the new marshal, Wyatt Earp. Wyatt, the man in the next room, had walked to King, yanked the iron from his hand, slapped his face, taken him by the scruff of the neck, and escorted him to city court. Meanwhile, back in Sweetwater some weeks later, Bat and Molly had late one night laid themselves out on the saloon's chuck-a-luck layout with amorous intent when, in a tantrum of jealous rage, the sergeant broke down the front door, apprised himself of the situation, and immediately slapped leather.

Bat broke off.

"Well?"

"It's not easy."

Birdie sat up so suddenly and in such frustration that her fruit almost fell. "Go on, damn you!"

"Well, first time he fired, Molly threw herself in front of me. Took the bullet in her stomach. The second shot got me, smashed my pelvis. But as I was going down, I drew and put one through his heart."

"That's right, you did—go on!"

Bat hid his face in the pillow. "You shouldn't do this to me, Birdie, even after all these years," he muffled. "I crawled to Molly. I held her in my arms. She hadn't long. She told me she loved me. Always would, even after death," he croaked. "Then—then—then she breathed her last on my lips."

"Oh God!"

And the stricken Birdie tore back the bedding and dived in and took his body and socks unto her and mingled her tears and limbs with his.

"You poor dear man!" she wailed. "You poor dear darling—Bat!"

Dyjean removed her blouse, skirt, shoes, hose, bloomers, corset, and then, standing with her back to him, unhooked a massive cotton brassiere, hung it over a bedpost, and turned.

"You have a beautiful body, Dyjean," Wyatt said.

"You really think so? Hey, how come you're not undressed? That's not fair."

He was in longjohns.

"There's something I want to say first."

"Say away—it's bed for me." She pulled down the covers and got in and sank practically out of sight. "Oh-oh, a feather tick. I guess they haven't got around to fixing this room up yet—you know, modern."

He sat on a chair near the bed, his back as straight as the back of the chair.

"You're a peculiar one," she said. "Still waters run deep, huh? When you ought to get down to brass tacks, you want to talk."

"You said a minute ago you just about believe I'm Wyatt Earp—which means not quite. In my opinion, girls shouldn't have sexual intercourse with men they don't know."

Her dander up, Dyjean sat up, covering her charms with bedclothing. "Are you saying I'm loose?"

"Loose is as loose does."

"You've got a nerve!"

"How can I prove who I am?"

"You don't have to prove anything!"

"You saw my gun. I knew considerable about Boot Hill. I'm the age Wyatt Earp would be now."

"I know." Dyjean pointed a finger. "I know—you won't come to bed because you're not capable any more!"

"I assure you I am."

"Prove it!"

The man in the chair shook his head. "I will—as soon as you accept me for myself."

She sank back into tick and pillow. "Oh Lord—are you stubborn."

"I'm a man of principle."

"You're a mule."

"Ask me anything about myself you care to."

"This is really cuckoo," Dyjean marveled. "The girl's in the bed and the guy gets fussy—I never. I sure haven't run into anything like this before." She heaved a rustic sigh. "Well, all right, fussbudget. Let's see. Wyatt Earp's got a brother Morgan."

"Did have. He's dead."

"Just trying to catch you. Where did he die?"

"Tombstone. Arizona Territory."

"How?"

"He was shot in the back."

"Go to the head of the class. See, I know—kids in Kansas grow up with these old stories. Tell me about it—let's see if you get it right."

"Must I?"

"Why not?"

"Speaking of it causes me pain."

"Sorry—this was your idea, Mister."

He sat near her in his longjohns, back as straight as the back of the chair. He spoke slowly, and Dyjean heard in his voice the pride of manhood and the pain which still accrued to his subject. After the carnage at the O.K. Corral in '81, after a thirty-day trial and a finding by Judge Spicer that Marshal Wyatt Earp, his brothers, Deputy Marshals Virgil and Morgan Earp, and Doc Holliday, defendants, were "fully justified in committing these homicides; that it was a necessary act done in the discharge of official duty"—after all this it was yet apparent that peace was not possible in Tombstone. The so-called "cowboy" faction, aided and abetted by Sheriff Behan, was resolved, rather than letting sleeping dogs lie, to be revenged on the victors. On December 29, nine days after Spicer's ver-

184

dict, Virgil Earp was ambushed, his left arm shattered by a bullet. On the night of March 20th next, Morgan Earp was playing billiards in Campbell & Hatch's parlor on Allen Street. Wyatt sat nearby, on guard. Chalking his cue, Morgan stood with his back to a rear door which opened on an alley. Pistols were fired through the glass panes in the door, plaster cut to bits near Wyatt's head, and Morgan fell. Wyatt carried his younger brother to a couch in Bob Hatch's office, and Dr. Goodfellow was called. A forty-five slug had entered the small of Morgan's back, severing the spine. "We know who did it, don't we, Wyatt?" Morgan whispered. Wyatt nodded. Morgan closed his eyes. In half an hour he was dead. He was thirty-one years of age.

Dyjean lay silently, wishing she'd never asked in the first place, but the man in the chair waited for her to play out the terrible string, to ask the last questions. She forced herself.

"What did you do?"

"Went after them."

"I know. And got them."

"Yes. It took a while."

"Who were they?"

"Indian Charlie. Curly Bill. Frank—"

"Stilwell," she finished for him. "In the railroad yard in Tucson."

"Yes." Then the man in the chair asked a question. "Are you satisfied, young lady?"

"Satisfied!" She began to cry. "I'm ashamed!"

"Don't be. That's all over, long ago. I don't speak of it often—only when I have to."

"I'm a bitch, a contrary bitch!" she sobbed. "How can I make it up to you?"

Now he was silent. Then she saw him standing by the

bed in the altogether, a fine figure of a man for his age, and he was smiling down at her.

"There's one way," he said, gently.

"Oh, yes!" Dyjean threw back the covers. "You boo-hoo-hop in here this minute, Wyatt Earp!"

"Aaaaah, yes." Bat relaxed, arms under his head, while Birdie slipped out of bed, brought him a Spud and matches and ashtray, and lit the cig for him.

"How will you think of me in the morning?" she asked, snuggling in again beside him.

"Fondly, my dear." He inhaled and exhaled a stream of self-congratulatory smoke. "Aaaaah, yes. Solid comfort."

"It's still hard," she sighed.

"No it isn't."

She giggled. "I mean, to believe. Who I'm actually in bed with."

"Sweetpea," said Bat, "you're a lucky girl."

"Lucky?"

"Are you ever. You've slept with Bat Masterson. You've rolled in the hay with history."

She thought about that.

The sounds of a catfight near the hotel intruded through the open window.

"My God!" gasped Birdie.

"What?"

"I just realized!"

"What?"

"Then that means—Dyjean must be in bed with the real Wyatt Earp!"

"Nobody but."

"I wonder if she knows!"

And on this contingency, an inspired Birdie flew the coop again, dragged a chair across the room to the door between 110 and 112, and stepped up on the chair to face the open transom.

"Gee, that was heavenly," sighed Dyjean.

"Indeed it was," Wyatt agreed. "If I do say so myself."

"What I don't get is, how'd you two happen to ask us out—me and Birdie?"

"Easy," replied the gallant Wyatt. "We thought you were the best-looking girls in town."

She lay close to him, arms about his neck. "The trouble is," she said, "I can't tell anybody I slept with the real Wyatt Earp. And even if I could—which I wouldn't—nobody'd believe me."

"Someday you can."

"When?"

"When you're a very old lady. You can tell your grandchildren, anybody, anything. That's one of the nice things about growing old."

"Well, maybe."

"Sure you can."

She thought about it.

The sounds of a catfight near the hotel intruded through the open window.

"Hey!" she said.

"Straw."

"Birdie's in bed with the real Bat Masterson!"

"Go to the head of the class."

"What if she doesn't know!"

And on this contingency, an inspired Dyjean jumped out of bed, dragged a chair across the room to the door between 110 and 112, and stepped up on the chair to the open transom.

Face to face, in excited whispers, cousin conferred with cousin through the transom.

In bed in 112, Bat stubbed his Spud, admired for a moment the splendor of Birdie's bare, moonlit ass up on the chair, and then, worn out after a long day of casing banks, cranking cars, riddling oilcans, drinking blue booze, and putting the blocks to a farmer's daughter, drifted off.

In bed in 110, Wyatt yawned, stretched, admired for a moment the amplitude of Dyjean's bare, moonlit ass mounted, as it were, on a pedestal, and fatigued after a long day trying to get Bat out of the bank, risking his neck in a horseless carriage, plinking practice, imbibing blue whiskey, reading ridiculous epitaphs, and indulging in amorous dalliance, drifted off.

Bat was roused by someone getting into bed with him.

"Hello, Mr. Masterson," said she.

It was Miss Dyjean Fedder.

"Well, well," said he. "What a pleasant surprise. But I don't think—"

"Ssssh," said she, cleaving to him. "Me and Birdie talked it over—we'll never have a chance like this again. So we snuck through the hall and switched rooms and beds. Now someday the both of us can brag we slept with the real Bat Masterson and the real Wyatt Earp—you know, when we're old. Won't that be something?"

"Oh," said Bat.

"You know, when we're old."

"But my dear young lady—"

"Really something!"

"I've had a hell of a hard day. At my age, what do you expect? I've already treated your cousin to a terrific—"

"Why, Mr. Masterson," said she, "I thought you carried a six-shooter!"

Wyatt was roused by someone getting into bed with him.

"Hello, Mr. Earp," said she.

It was Miss Birdie Fedder.

"Howdy, ma'am," said he. "Well, well. How did this come about?"

She tied him down with a strong arm and an eager leg. "Well, I told Dyjean. Bat told me how lucky I was—you know, sleeping with him."

"He did, did he?"

"History and all that. So I told Dyjean, we better make hay while the sun shines—then we'll both have been to bed with the real Bat Masterson and the real Wyatt Earp. So there she is and here I am!"

"I see."

"You don't turn down second helpings, do you?"

189

"I didn't used to."

Pssssssssst!"

It was a man in dire straits at the transom over the door between the rooms.

"Will you excuse me, young lady?" asked Wyatt.

"Sure, Mr. Earp," said Birdie. "Just don't leave me up the creek."

Wyatt climbed out of bed, moved to the door, and stepped up on the chair.

Standing on the chairs, their voices low, their bare, moon-lit, legendary asses displayed to the admiring maidens as though in a museum, the two gentlemen chewed the rag through the transom.

"Who the hell's idea was this!" Bat demanded.

"You and your history," Wyatt reminded.

"We shouldn't take advantage of these girls."

"A kind heart never helps at poker."

"Goddammit!"

"Aren't you up to it?"

"Damn right I am! But I'm saddle-sore!" Bat hissed. "And we've got a big day tomorrow!"

"You know what they say in New York."

"New York?"

" 'It's a great life if you don't weaken.' "

At five minutes before ten o'clock in the morning of 5th May they park the Ford Touring Sedan at the curb on

190

Railroad Avenue a few feet from the corner. Both are crabby as bears with sore paws this morning after, and a difference of opinion flares. Mr. Earp orders his driver to leave the engine running. Mr. Masterson objects that a car parked with the engine running is sure to attract notice. Mr. Earp counters that he, Mr. Masterson, based on his performance yesterday, has as much chance as a snowball in hell of starting the car fast enough for a successful getaway. Mr. Masterson declares that he is the driver, he will make all decisions relative to the car, and his decision is to cut the engine. Mr. Earp reminds him that he, Mr. Earp, is calling the play, and the term "play" as used in the West is all-inclusive—therefore the engine will be left running. Mr. Masterson asks if he, Mr. Earp, would care to have an ebony eye. Mr. Earp replies that if he, Mr. Masterson, cannot recall his, Mr. Earp's, prowess with his fists from their early buffalo-hunt days he, Mr. Earp, will be only too glad to escort him on a trip down Memory Lane. Mr. Earp then turns and strides around the corner. After a minute of meditation Mr. Masterson follows, allowing the Ford's four cylinders to continue functioning.

"Not sure I'm up to this," Bat grumbles.

"You better be."

"What a night!"

They wait across the street from the Drovers Bank of Dodge City, its white glazed brick facade sparkling in the morning sun.

"Well," says Bat, "you tried 'em both. Which one wins the Bible?"

"Bible?"

"In bed, I mean. Birdie or Dyjean?"

"We've got work to do."

This morning three men and a woman wait at the doors for the bank to open.

"Slip your gun," Wyatt mutters. "Make sure it draws easy."

Reaching under jackets, they slip guns out of and back into holsters.

"You take the left side, the tellers," Wyatt orders. "I'll handle the right—and get Beanstone out of his office. Masks on as soon as we get through the doors."

"I say a toss-up."

"What?"

"Birdie and Dyjean. Sweet patooties, both of 'em."

They'd bought bandannas at a drygoods store, tying them round their necks under jackets, ready to raise.

"Last chance to change our minds," says Bat.

"Your mind."

Bat angles his derby up and down, this way and that. "I'm in. We drew aces last night—never leave the game when the cards are coming, I say."

"No shooting unless we have to."

"Okeh."

"But if you have to, hit something."

"Okeh."

Tempus fidgets. The local yokels before the bank doors bustle a bit. The doors are unlocked. The yokels yank them open.

"Let's go," says Wyatt.

"Leave a light in the window, Mother, I'll be home late tonight!"

They cross the street.

They climb the steps, open the doors.

They enter the bank. People moving, people standing, people sitting, people looking. They reach under jackets to raise bandannas.

At this instant there occurs the one thing, the one event, the one coincidence that no one sane of mind in the world would have expected or predicted or believed could possibly occur.

Behind them, a gun goes off.

Plaster showers from the ceiling.

Behind them, simultaneously, a shout—"Everybody on the floor! This is a holdup!"

Incredibly confounded, W.B. Masterson and W.B.S. Earp fall in slow motion to the floor.

"Goddammit, we said on the floor! That means you and you—and you! On the floor and you move and we'll blow your goddam heads off!"

A gun goes off again.

Faint cries, from women and from men.

On his side, facing W.B.S. Earp, lies W.B. Masterson. The expression on his phiz is indescribable.

On his side, facing W.B. Masterson, lies W.B.S. Earp. The expression on his phiz is indescribable.

The Drovers Bank of Dodge City is being robbed this morning, this minute, by someone else.

The sound of shoes, running. Voices. Of a woman sobbing hysterically. Drawers being hauled open. A metal box dropped. Something, a wastebasket perhaps, overturned. Voices hollow in the vault.

193

W.B. and W.B.S. turtle heads. There are two men, maybe three. Bareheaded. One is bald. Denim workshirts and pants, and across their mugs, narrow strips of black leather with holes for eyes. Professionals. They carry handguns, small-calibre and snub-nosed.

A shout—"All right! You-all stay on the floor and don't move for five minutes—five minutes or you'll be goddam sorry you did!"

A gunshot for an exclamation mark.

Plaster showers.

The front doors bang.

Three ticks of a clock.

Lungs let loose.

Men shout.

Women shriek.

Furniture crashes.

An alarm bell rings.

Amid the commotion W.B. Masterson and W.B.S. Earp rise and make rapidly for the doors.

"We'll get 'em!" yells W.B. Masterson.

They tear out of the bank just in time.

Around the corner a dark green Studebaker Touring Sedan, its top down, two men in front, two men in the rear, lurches out of sight, evidently headed east.

They leg it across the street and round the corner toward the faithful Ford.

"'We'll get 'em!'" pants a furious Wyatt. "What in hell did you say that for!"

"Damifino!" pants a bewildered Bat. "Habit!"

"I know why I said it!"

"Yeah?"

"We gotta get 'em! They got our money!"

They roar and rattle, shake and shimmy down the narrow macadam road running east from Dodge, the same road they had taken yesterday for driving and target practice, hats jammed down over ears, Bat bent over the wheel in imitation of Barney Oldfield, Wyatt on the edge of the seat holding on to the windshield frame. Spark and throttle levers are advanced to the utmost. The needle of the Stewart speedometer stands at forty mph, full speed. The red line of the Boyce Moto-Meter on the radiator has risen to "High Efficiency."

Gradually, however, the prey draws away. The 1916 Studebaker has been endowed this model year with a new four-cylinder, 3 $\frac{7}{8}$ bore × 5-in. stroke engine which, according to newspaper advertisements, endows the car with "Brute Power." Horsepower has been upped to forty— double the brute power of the Model T—and top speed to sixty mph. And so the Studie draws away, half a mile away, three-quarters of a mile away.

Then a lucky break. It must slow to a crawl behind a lumbering Mogul tractor, cannot pass on the right because the shoulder is too narrow, nor on the left because a farmer with a wagonload of agriculture bars the passing lane.

Bat pounds in elation on the steering wheel. But then, as they come within a city block, close enough to identify the heads of the four thugs, two in front, two in the rear, one of these bald, tractor and wagon pass in opposite directions and the way is cleared for the Studebaker, which spurts around the Mogul and once again extends its lead.

"Goddammit!" rages Bat. "I told you we should've got a Hudson Super-Six!"

Now they can see, down the road on the horizon, the leafy bower and elevator tower which is Garden of Eden. And now they can hear, in their rear, the keening of a siren. It is of course that of Peace Officer Harvey Wadsworth, mounted on his Indian Powerplus, in full hue and cry after the criminals. Siren screaming, he whizzes by the Tin Lizzie as though it were standing still, bending low over the handlebars and doing the factory-guaranteed seventy-three-plus mph, hat blown from his head, goggles over his eyes, the expression on his cherubic cheeks carved by wind into one of superhuman concentration. Opportunity may knock but once, young Harvey knows, and surely this is the biggest bang of his career.

Bat and Wyatt watch as the motorcycle closes the gap. The dark green sedan seems to slow in response to the siren. There are tiny flashes of light from it—gunfire. The Indian careens off the highway and plows into a fence and through the fence, where it somersaults into corn which will be knee-high by the Fourth of July. Like a child's toy, a jumping-jack, the rider's body jumps twenty feet in the air on impact with the fence, then drops to earth to lie in a sprawl of blood, broken bones, and baby blue.

This cuts the comedy. This changes the water on the min-
nows. Bat and Wyatt pass the remains of the peace officer,
snatch glances at them, then at each other. Bat's gray eyes
glitter. Wyatt's face is grim, his eyes a cold and lethal blue.
Harvey Wadsworth wore a badge. He was what they were
long ago. Now he has been gunned down in the performance of his duty, and they have failed in theirs. Progress
has made it impossible for them to back his play. In the
old days lawmen backed lawmen to the death. Many the
time, shotguns at the ready, Bat and Wyatt and Charlie
Bassett and Bill Tilghman and Jim Masterson and Morgan
Earp covered rear doors and side streets and back alleys
for each other when one was in a tight. That was another
century, however, a simple century, and these two perfect,
gentle knights in the Model T have lived beyond that time,
into a new and unnatural. They could not have covered
Harvey Wadsworth—blame it on the infernal combustion
engine. But are they whipped? Not by a long shot. Are
they too deef to hear the wolf howl, too mossbacked to
make their own play? Hell, no. And so, full of fight, they
forget the why and wherefore of the morning, the long
trail by train into their past, and its purpose; they lay aside
the subject of the loot. If they could not stop the taking of
a life, they can at least, by God, avenge it.

The chase continues. The road over the prairie is straight
as the part in a bartender's hair. Again the Studie and its
four villains draw away from the flivver and its two-man
posse. Wyatt twists in the seat, bends his angular frame
over the seat back, reaches to the floor of the rear com-

partment, and comes up with his ancient buffalo gun, the one he had taken from its glass case in the Beeson Museum in exchange for forty dollars—the great .50-calibre Sharp's. Standing the rifle upright, he searches a pocket, finds the single three-inch-long cartridge which had been exhibited with the gun, and loads it. With this very blunderbuss, when in his twenties, he had earned his living with feats of marksmanship and mountains of hides which had earned him, in turn, the envy of every hunter and skinner between the Arkansas and the Canadian.

He plants his left knee on the seat, hoists himself, leans forward, lays the long barrel of the Sharp's across the top of the windshield, shoulders the rifle, and braces himself with right foot on the floorboard and left elbow on the windshield.

"Blow out a tire!" yells Bat.

"I intend to!"

Wyatt Earp takes aim. At forty mph the Ford roars and rattles, shakes and shimmies. The range is half a mile. Just then the red line on the Boyce Moto-Meter rises to "Danger—Steaming!" and a plume of steam gushes from the radiator, obscuring vision. The shot cannot be made.

Bat sucks his breath.

The one, the only Wyatt Earp fires.

The report splits the eardrums.

Half a mile down the road the sedan veers, slows, veers, slows, and wobbles. The rear right-hand tire throws strips of rubber. Then the Studebaker disappears from view in Garden of Eden.

The Ford full-steams ahead until, as it nears civilization, Bat cuts the engine and lets the vehicle coast to a stop in the shade of the first tree. They get out of the car.

"They'll hunt a hole," says Wyatt over the whistle of steam. "They've got a lame animal."

"They're in there, all right," Bat agrees.

"Well, let's find 'em."

They raise hats and draw guns, then start together at a measured pace into Garden of Eden.

It is even less than a village—half a dozen small frame houses secluded in high cottonwoods and sycamores and Chinese elms on the left side of the road. They see an old woman's face at a window. An old man emerges from an outhouse, buckling his belt. In a front yard two children play, a boy and a girl, and, at the sight of two men striding down the center of the road with guns in hands, a comely young woman hurries into the yard and clucks her chicks into the house. Bat smiles and tips her a polite derby.

They approach a general store with a gas pump out front on the same side of the road as the houses. They walk more slowly now, in and out of sunshine, in and out of shade, old Colts swinging at their sides. Except for blackbirds in the trees and robins in the grass they walk in silence, as though Garden of Eden, interested more in fiction than in fact, is sleeping late. It is a fair, fresh spring morning.

"Here we go again," says Bat, bemused. "Gathering nuts in May."

"Hold it," says Wyatt.

They stop.

On the right side of the road, opposite the houses and general store, a hundred yards away, there are no trees. Instead, rising higher than any tree, visible for miles around, rears the tower of a grain elevator, railroad spur line running beside it at the rear. The elevator is painted pure white, and below its top, in blue capitals, is lettered "GARDEN OF EDEN CO-OP."

"There," says Wyatt. "Behind."

"They've gotta change that tire," says Bat. "Two on the tire, I bet, and two lookouts."

"Um. Let's see if we draw fire."

"Okeh."

They walk again, toward the elevator.

Ninety yards, eighty yards, and they are fired on, one warning round apparently from the side of the tower, and missed by a mile. They neither flinch nor falter, but walk on at a left oblique, keeping the tower between them and the men behind it.

There are a thousand and more grain elevators in Kansas, like as peas in a pod and called, in the vernacular of the grade trade, "bins." They are cylindrical and built of concrete, with walls eight inches thick. They stand eighty to ninety feet high. The diameter of a bin is approximately fifteen feet, the circumference forty-seven. The sole function of such a structure is storage. Wagons or trucks loaded with wheat or corn are driven from the fields to the bins and weighed at the "scalehouse" by the "scaleman" to determine the weight, hence the number of bushels, of the load. The wagon or truck is then moved over a grated pit, the sides of the vehicle are removed, and the grain is shoveled into the pit, where a power-driven "belt leg" lifts it to the top of the bin and dumps it in. The average elevator stores approximately eighteen thousand bushels, or nineteen million pounds. When orders to ship grain are received by the cooperative, boxcars are shunted along the spur line and positioned by the elevator. Car doors are slid open, "grain doors" or planks eight feet long and eighteen inches high are laid atop one another inside the open doors to prevent spillage, and the long "unload spout" of galvanized steel, built into the elevator, is swung over and down and into the car and opened. Grain flows by gravity into the boxcar, which holds two thousand bushels. When the car is full, doors are shut and the next car moved to the unload spout. The bin of the Garden of Eden Co-Op is on this dramatic day in May filled to far less than its capacity with two thousand plus bushels of wheat known as "hard winter red," the pride of Kansas and a variety invaluable in the milling of flour.

Bat and Wyatt reach the wall of the elevator. Wyatt nods to the right, indicates that he will take the left, and revolvers raised, backs tight to the wall, they inch along the concrete, moving in opposite directions round the mighty mulberry bush.

At the edge of his left eye Bat can perceive the rear half of the Studebaker, parked in behind the bin. It is raised two feet off the ground. They've had time to jack it up by the bumper, but not enough to pry off the tatters of the tire and install the spare. He squats. Under the sedan, on the far side, he spots pantlegs and a pair of black brogans. He eases erect, crosses his chest with the Colt, aims at the jack from forty feet, and fires. The jack whangs from the bumper, the car comes down with a thud, exposing a head on the far side, and Bat fires again, instantly, drilling the thug between the eyes. He crashes on his back. Astonished and delighted by his accuracy, Bat bounces toward the sedan like a boy, out and away from the protection of the elevator.

He'd be perforated, but Wyatt, stalking round the other side of the tower, sees a man near the top of a ladder leaning against the wall aim a .38 automatic at the unsuspecting Bat, and yells. Distracted, the crook fires and misses, allowing Wyatt the split second needed to get off a snap shot which hits him squarely. The man drops his pistol. Wyatt comes out of concealment. The man on the ladder reaches into his shirt as though for another weapon, and deliberately Wyatt puts a second slug in him. Still he does not fall from the ladder. To the amazement of the two spectators, he begins slowly to descend the ladder, rung by rung.

He is a gross crook, broadshouldered and bullnecked and bald as a hen's egg, and, despite his agony, despite the internal damage done by the two doses of lead, he continues to come down the wooden ladder, which is at least eighteen feet long and stands against the wall with its upper end propped just below a manhole with a hinged

202

iron cover. Bat and Wyatt stare at him. He turns his head to speak.

"You're not cops," he groans. "Not your business."

"We made it ours," says Wyatt. "Where's the other two?"

"Where's the money?" asks Bat.

Rung by rung Baldy descends, turning to see Bat. "Who the hell're you?"

"Bat Masterson. That's Wyatt Earp."

"Like shit," groans Baldy, lets go of the ladder, slides the last rungs, and hits the ground dead as a carp in a cup of spit.

Bat and Wyatt approach the varmint, stand over him, stare down at him.

"That's two for Harvey Wadsworth," says Wyatt. "Two to go."

"He didn't believe us either, the dumb son-of-a-bitch," says a scornful Bat. "Who else did he think could shoot like this?"

They proceed to the Studebaker to inspect the yegg Bat has deceased. The hole between his eyes is neat as a pin.

"My God, look at that!" Bat exclaims.

"What is it?"

"That, my friend, is a tommy gun."

It lies beside the yegg—short stock and barrel, round steel drum attached below the point where stock ends and barrel begins, turnkey in the center of the drum. The words "Auto Ordnance Corp. Col. Thomas Thompson" are stamped into the drum.

"I've never seen one, but I've heard of 'em," says Bat.

"The latest thing. Developed for the Army—but crooks would have 'em first, of course. I expect Rothstein and his hoods have a-plenty. So these guys were real pros—prob'ly from Kansas City or somewhere."

"How does it work?"

"Also called a submachine gun. Forty-five calibre, spring-loaded. Well, that drum holds fifty rounds in a clip. Jam in the drum, wind up the key, hold the trigger, and you get off fifty rounds faster'n you can say Jack Robinson."

Wyatt holsters his Peacemaker and picks up the weapon.

"Hold it like a baby," warns Bat. "Good thing I got this bastard before he could open up. He'd have cut me to pieces."

Wyatt is studying the elevator and the long ladder under the manhole. "They must be inside—the other two. And the money."

"Or over there in the trees, on the lam."

"Only one way to find out." Wyatt points. "Why don't you shinny up that ladder and open the cover on that manhole. Easy like. If they're in there, they'll let you know."

Bat backs off. "Oh, no. I can't stand heights. I can't even get up on a stepladder."

"O.K." Wyatt hands over the tommy gun and starts for the ladder.

Bat follows, reaching apologetically into his jacket. "Here—use this or they'll take your fingers off."

Wyatt accepts the ruler with its maxim, "A Penny Saved Is A Penny Earned," steps over Baldy's body, and mounts the ladder.

Bat is glad to wait and spectate. "That Millie Sughrue," he recalls. "What a looker!"

It is an eighteen-foot ladder. The manhole has enough diameter to admit someone to clean the bottom of the bin—presumably its purpose—and a hinged lid or cover which is open a crack, perhaps to let in light. Keeping an eye on the cover, Wyatt climbs just high enough to reach with his right arm, to insert the ruler under the cover, and with a flick of his hand to swing it open wide.

It's like busting a hornets' nest. A blast of gunfire blows a spread of bullets through the hole, shredding the ruler and causing Wyatt to duck instinctively even though he's shielded by eight inches of concrete.

Carefully he comes down the ladder. Together, he and Bat sidle out of range at the base of the tower.

"You were right, all right," Bat admits.

"Wish I wasn't."

"Damn 'em."

"We've got a bearcat by the tail. And we don't have time to wait 'em out." Wyatt frowns and rearranges some splayed hairs in his mustache. "Everybody in Dodge knows the bank's been hit by now, and Harvey went after 'em— this way. Any minute now, half the town'll be here—at least whatever law they've got left. Maybe the county sheriff and deputies."

Bat, too, studies the elevator. "Talk about holed up.

How to get at 'em, or get 'em out. Tougher than lobster out of a shell."

Wyatt nods, then does a double take. "That's it."

"What's it?"

"I know how. You just said it. Bat, we're going up that big pecker—to the top. Look." With an arm Wyatt follows a row of iron rungs built into the wall of the elevator all the way from ground level to the top—eighty or ninety feet. Bat goes white as a sheet. "It's the only way," Wyatt asserts.

"The hell you say!"

"Listen—on the other side of that wall are two more murdering bastards and fifty, sixty thousand dollars— d'you want 'em or not?"

"I know, but my God—"

"What'd we come to Kansas for—learn how to drive a car?"

Bat shakes his head. "Wyatt, I'd never make it," he implores. "I'd fall. And whatta we do when we're up there? I don't get it."

"I'll tell you on top. Let's go."

"You tell me now!"

"Trust me."

"Goddammit!"

Rrrriiiipppppp!

Halfway up, Bat first, Wyatt a close second for support, the one, the only Bat Masterson rips off a tremendous fart of fear in his friend's face.

"Damn you," growls Wyatt.

"I can't help it! I'm scared!"

"Keep going."

"I just remembered—we gotta climb down!"

"You shoot another rabbit, I'll see to it you're down damn fast."

Before starting the ascent, Wyatt had pulled his belt from its loops and belted the tommy gun to his side. He'd had Bat reload both revolvers, holster one and stick the other under his belt.

Near the top Bat stops. "No, no, I can't. Wyatt, I'm finished."

"Don't look down."

"I'm weak as a cat. After last night, this is too much for me. A man my age—"

Wyatt reaches up and raps him in the rump with a fist. "Onward and upward."

"Oh my God."

Wyatt raps him again.

Bat moves, but slowly. "I wish I was anywhere but here—even Grogan's." He stops.

Wyatt raps him again.

Bat moves, but slowly. "How I ever let you talk me into coming way out here in the sticks I'll never know. I could be hoisting one with the boys on Broadway, I could be safe at home with my dear wife, I—"

"Shuddup and giddup."

They reach the rim of the great cylinder and crawl onto the flat top. Bat stands, sways, Wyatt holds him, and they look out over the Lord's majestic pool table, which is Kansas. Above them, puffing along like farm implements, little white clouds till blue and heavenly fields. From this vantage they command also, it seems, the entire U.S. of A., from the Catskills over the Rockies all the way to the Sierra Nevada. They scout the black highway arrowing through verdant green from Garden of Eden, below, to the trees and church steeples of Dodge. There is no unusual traffic on the road, which means no pursuit of the bankrobbers has yet been organized. Wyatt turns Bat by an elbow toward a large open manhole near the far edge, cover lying beside it.

"Keep your voice down," he mutters. "See that hole? Maybe a ladder down there, inside, I dunno. Anyway, that's my idea. Ricochet."

"Ricochet?"

"You made me think of it, mentioning lobster. The night in that restaurant we were eating lobster—I recollect shell flying all over the place. Ricochet."

"Oh, sure." Bat unties his bandanna and mops his brow. "That shoot-out I had in Dodge with Peacock and Updegraff, in '81. Ricochet took a newspaper right out of a guy's hands reading it in Dr. McCarty's drugstore. Slugs'll do funny things."

Wyatt unbelts the machine gun. "O.K., they're down there in the grain under us, way down, near that hole by the ladder. We can't go in after 'em, they can't come out on account of us—but they don't know we're up here. So what we do, we unload our artillery down that hole—fifty rounds in this tommy gun, twelve in your pistols. At an angle, so the rounds hit the ceement going down and ricochet every whichway. Sixty-two slugs—odds are pretty good we'll put some holes in 'em. Should be like shooting fish in a barrel."

Bat nods. "You said it. Wonderful. Okeh, gimme the tommy gun."

"Nope. I carried it up."

"You don't know anything about it."

"Neither do you. Besides, you had a hard night last night—I had a dandy. C'mon. You go for the other side of the hole, I'll take this—we'll mow those boys down. Now don't make any noise, and as soon as we're there, cut loose. I mean cut loose."

"Well, okeh. That clip wound tight?"

Wyatt tries the turnkey. "Yup."

Bat unholsters the .45 from his shoulder and unlimbers its mate from his belt. "You sure you can handle that thing?"

"Don't get funny," Wyatt deadpans. "'Smile when you say that, stranger.'"

They tiptoe to the hole, Bat taking the far side, Wyatt the near. Wyatt falls to his knees and shoulders the Thompson and depresses the muzzle into the hole at an angle and pulls the trigger and holds it as Bat, bending over, empties the Colt in each hand at the inside wall of the bin on the opposite side. It's like shooting blind into a deep dark well. The barrel of the submachine gun, like those of all rapid-fire weapons when on automatic, tends to rise, and Wyatt must exert real effort to keep it down. The sixty-two reports meld into one continuous explosion, the echo of which, when the firing has ceased, booms and booms back and forth from one interior wall of the elevator to the other.

Bat and Wyatt remain in place until, at last, the huge bin beneath them is silent as the grave.

Bat rises, removes his hat, and hangs it solemnly over his heart. "Keno."

Wyatt rises. "Two more for Harvey."

"Now by God the money."

Evidencing not the least terror of height on the trip down the iron rungs, Bat talks a blue streak about the lovely loot and the splash he'll make blowing his share when he hits good old Gotham again, and when they reach terra firma he hurries ahead of Wyatt and whooshes up the wooden ladder like a Hottentot after a coconut and sticks his head fearlessly through the manhole.

"Well?" Wyatt inquires, leaning the tommy gun against the wall and commencing his own climb.

Bat withdraws his head and beams. "Got 'em. Great shooting—we never miss, do we? Mind if I go first, Mr. Earp?"

"Age before beauty."

Bat dives through the hole like a twelve-year-old and presently has company. There is ample light inside, provided both by the manhole and the larger aperture on top of the bin through which they have just hurled lightning bolts of lead. They pay scant heed to the two stiffs near the far wall, riddled apparently by ricochet, but begin at once to tromp in circles, ankle-deep in wheat.

"Where in hell!" yelps Bat, his words reverberating in the bin.

"Maybe under 'em," offers Wyatt.

They turn the two stiffs over, but there is nothing underneath—coins, currency, bank bags.

"It's gotta be in here!" cries Bat. "It's not in the car—I

looked! Goddam 'em—where'd they stash it?"

Wyatt rubs his chin.

Then it breaks on Bat. "Oh, no!" he mourns. "They buried it—the bastards buried it!"

He throws himself to his knees and burrows like a badger, emitting a stream of wheat behind him. "Dig, dammit, dig!"

A sober Wyatt goes to his knees to delve with both hands. "Must be a couple thousand bushels in here," he says. "Like looking for a—"

"Don't give me that needle crap!" rages Bat. "Just dig, goddammit, dig!"

"Mornin'," says a face in the manhole.

Startled out of their socks, they look up from their labors. Of all the bum luck, it's a man in a miller's cap, a middle-aged hick with the jawbone of an ass and consumed with curiosity.

"Morning," says Wyatt.

"Morning," says Bat.

"You boys sayin' your prayers?"

"Dropped a nickel," Bat explains.

"Like lookin' for a needle in a haystack. Who might you be?"

"I might be Bat Masterson. This might be Wyatt Earp. Who're you?"

"Well, I might be Napoleon Bonapartey. Would you b'lieve that?"

"I might not."

"Work for the co-op," says the face. "I'm the scaleman. L.D. Good."

211

"L.D.? What's that stand for?"

"Nothin'. My name is all. L.D."

There is a lull. Good looks at them and they look at Good and hope he will go away.

"Say, d'you fellers know there's two dead men out here?"

"You don't say," says Bat in despair.

The scaleman sticks his head through the hole. "God Almighty, two more in here."

"Two and two makes four," says Bat.

"God Almighty. Thought I was runnin' a grain bin, not a funeral parlor."

Wyatt takes over. "They robbed the bank in Dodge this morning."

"You don't say."

"We chased after 'em and caught 'em here. They weren't inclined to give up peaceably."

"Well, I swan," says L.D. Good. "I live cross the way, and it sounded like a war so I come over."

"Thanks a lot," says Bat.

"Well, now you got 'em, what d'you propose to do with 'em? After you find your nickel, that is."

"Take 'em back to Dodge," says Wyatt. "Will you lend us a hand?"

"Sure thing. How?"

Wyatt rises. "First get off the ladder. Then we'll pitch 'em out the hole. We've got a car at the edge of town. We'll drive it in and you can help us load up and we'll be off."

"Sure thing." L.D. Good has one last gape at the riddled crooks. "God Almighty," says he, and disappears.

Bat staggers up out of the wheat. "Take 'em back to Dodge? Are you crazy?"

Wyatt dusts himself. "I am not. We're stuck now—we've got to brazen it out. We haul 'em to Dodge, then, when the ruckus has died down, we skin back here and find the cash—it's got to be in this grain somewhere. Then we keep going and split up in Wichita. You head east and I head west and that's all she wrote."

"They won't believe us in a month of Sundays! What'll we say?"

"I'll think of something."

Bat glares at him.

"Say," interjects L.D. Good, reappearing. "How many times you expect me to go up'n down this ladder? I ain't no monkey."

Ooooo-gah! Ooooo-gah!

Bat pumps the hand-operated brass-belled Klaxon horn on the Ford as they enter Dodge City.

"Why in hell do that?" Wyatt wants to know.

"Blowing our own horn! Masterson and Earp bring home the bacon again!"

"Earp and Masterson!"

Ooooo-gah! Ooooo-gah!

The horn moos and the T chugs and Bat has hit it on the nose—they are indeed bringing home the bad guys as in days of yore. Two of the bank robbers and their weapons they have dumped into the rear compartment. The other two, one of them Baldy, they have draped over the hood of the sedan. And as they fanfare into town with the trophies of the chase, a Chalmers pulls in behind them, then a Maxwell, then a Hudson, then an old lady in an electric, then a Big Bull tractor, then an ice-wagon after these, all honking and hollering, plus a smatter of small boys skipping alongside, and, by the time they roll along

Front Street, all they lack to be a parade is a brass band, a couple of clowns, and enough horseshit to require a shovel.

Ooooo-gah! Ooooo-gah!

The Klaxon clears a way through the milling crowd in front of the Drovers Bank and, riding tall in the saddle, Mr. Earp and Mr. Masterson arrive. A cheer goes up, two men bustle down the steps, and our heroes dismount.

"Great work, boys," says one of the two men, who wears a tin star. "I'm Jack Sughrue, sheriff of Ford County— my daughter-in-law works in the bank here. I got here late—been up to Spearville and just got the word. You see anything of Harvey Wadsworth, our peace officer?"

Mssrs. Earp and Masterson remove hats. "Sorry to tell you," says Masterson. "He came after these mugs and they shot him off his bike. He's dead. You'll find him off the road near Garden of Eden."

A hush falls over Front Street. There is scarcely a dry eye.

"Sorry to hear it," says the sheriff. "Harvey was a good boy. Well, we'll go out and get 'im." Sughrue has a closer look at one of the corpses over the hood of the Ford. "Baldy Timms," says he. "Out of Kansas City—got a record a mile long. They were professionals, all right, this bunch. How'd you stop 'em?"

"We blew out one of their tires," says Masterson modestly. "They pulled into Garden of Eden and weren't inclined to come along peaceably, so we had it out with 'em. They changed their minds."

"They sure did," says the sheriff. "Two against four— how 'bout that, folks?"

Loud huzzahs from the admiring throng, after which the portly well-dressed gent who'd accompanied Sughrue introduces himself with a ham hand.

214

"William J. Beanstone, gentlemen. President and Cashier. Bill Beanstone to you—I am honored and privileged to shake your hands. One thing I'm bound to ask, though—begging your pardon—no offense meant—where is the blessed money?"

This one Mr. Earp, who's been cogitating, takes it upon himself to answer. "No sign of it anywhere. My hunch is, after I blew out their tire, and they knew the jig was up, they threw it out along the road somewhere—got rid of the evidence."

"Just out of curiosity," inquires Mr. Masterson, "how much did they grab?"

All and sundry are all ears.

"Ahem." Bill Beanstone speaks with a gravity suitable to his subject. "We're insured, of course. Ahem. By our best accounting, in the neighborhood of fifty to sixty thousand."

"That's a nice neighborhood," nods Mr. Masterson with a glance at Mr. Earp. "A damn shame, sir. Well, you look along that roadside, you'll break an ankle on it."

Overhearing this, the fringes of the crowd fall away, and the affairs of a large number of solid citizens seem to require their presence elsewhere.

"For God's sake, Jack," says banker to sheriff behind his hand, "will you get your ass out on the road while that money's still there?"

"Oh. Sure will, Bill." Sheriff Sughrue mobilizes himself. "We'll pick up Harvey, too."

"The cash first."

"Sure." He waves at the four criminal corpses, two in the car, two over the hood. "What'll I do with this meat? Undertake it?"

"Later. Leave 'em be for now. Be a great thing for the tourists." He turns to Mr. Earp and Mr. Masterson. "Now gentlemen, step into the bank, if you please. We have business to transact."

He leads the way, they follow, as does half the throng, up the steps and into the marbled hall of the Drovers Bank of Dodge City. "Excuse me a moment, I have to make a long-distance telephone call," says he, and betakes himself into his office.

Mr. Earp and Mr. Masterson are surrounded by well-wishers and hero worshippers, and little wonder. Every soul present has been brought up on blood and thunder. Dodge had been the "Cowboy Capitol of the World." Dodge had been the "Beautiful, Bibulous Babylon of the Frontier." Dodge has been determined to profit from its past while it could. The catch is, the blood has run a trifle thin, the thunder has shrunk to a hiccup, and the past is irrecoverably past, so that for too many decades now the town has rocked on the front porch of the West like a painted crone, cackling lore, gumming memory, and existing on the charity of brave men long departed. Thanks to these two strangers, however, this day of 5th May in 1916 is a whangdoodle. Every denizen of Dodge appreciates in pulse and pocketbook what they have done. Whoever they may be, the out-of-towners have turned back the clock, God bless 'em, and made of Dodge a naughty girl again. Why, the sound of the six-gun has again been heard! There are four fresh kills on Front Street! Why, this may even call for four new headboards on Boot Hill!

Mr. Masterson spots Millie Sughrue at a teller's window, tips his hat, and is repaid with roseate cheeks. A stringbean, a callow lad of twenty or so in a straw boater with a "Press" card in the band, moves in on the guests of honor with pad and pencil and an earnest expression.

"Yessir, gents, I'm Dudley Robison of the Dodge City

Daily Globe—like to ask you a few questions."

"At your service, Dud," says the amiable Mr. Masterson. "Always glad to cooperate with the press."

"What I want," says the stringbean, pencil posed, "is the gory details of the shoot-out. What a story! Nothing like this around here since the old Earp and Masterson days. 'Showdown in Garden of Eden!' 'Dodge City Alive And Kicking!' It'll make the front page everywhere—even New York City!"

"Sounds swell," says Mr. Masterson.

"But I've gotta know how you did it, and where. Oh, yes, and your names and addresses, and what you're doing in town, and—"

"Tomorrow," says Mr. Masterson. "Let's make it tomorrow morning, shall we?"

"Sorry, sir, my deadline's tonight. Now let's get to the facts. First off, who are you?"

"Tomorrow," smiles Mr. Masterson, delivering a swift kick to Dudley Robison's shins as banker Beanstone emerges from his office with a broad smile.

"Gentlemen, I have splendid news!" He lays ham hands on their shoulders. "Just telephoned Topeka—the State Banking Association. We offer a reward for the apprehension and conviction of bank robbers in the fair state of Kansas—well, you've apprehended 'em all right—and we won't need to convict 'em! Therefore it gives me great pleasure to inform you that I am authorized by the Association to remit the reward immediately—now!"

"Much obliged," says Mr. Earp.

"How much?" says the blunt Mr. Masterson.

"Five thousand dollars!"

The bank buzzes. Mr. Earp and Mr. Masterson appear to be highly gratified.

"I assume you'll share and share alike," says Bill Bean-stone. "Now if you'll just give me your names, I'll issue checks at once."

"Our names?" asks Mr. Masterson.

Mr. Earp again steps into the breach. "Beanstone, you have us up a tree. The fact is, we are Wells-Fargo agents, on assignment hereabouts. We're not allowed to use our real names. The company—"

"You wouldn't have the cash, would you?" Mr. Masterson asks the banker.

"The cash? Well, matter of fact, I do. The thieves over-looked one box in the vault—twelve thousand in it. If you'll chance carrying five thousand—"

"We'll chance it," declares Mr. Earp.

"Very well, if you say. Just one moment." And the banker heads for the vault.

"Wells-Fargo agents?"

This is Dudley Robison, the newshawk.

"That's right, my boy," says Mr. Masterson.

"Well, that's a corker, too!" exclaims the pestiferous youth, poking pencil behind ear. "Let's talk about that a minute!"

"Tomorrow, Dud," smiles Mr. Masterson.

"What time?"

"Shall we say six ayem?"

"In the morning?"

"I'm an early riser."

"Six o'clock!"

"Early to bed, too."

"Here we are, gentlemen!" Wm. J. Beanstone plows into the humanity and presents each of the honorees with a crisp packet of currency. "Would you care to count?"

"No, sir," laughs Mr. Masterson.

"No, sir," says Mr. Earp, and then, with a bee in his

bonnet, "By the way, sir, did the late Harvey Wadsworth leave a family?"

Beanstone lengthens his face. "I regret to say, he did. A lovely wife, a little girl."

"Ah," says Mr. Earp. "In that case, my friend and I would like to contribute five hundred apiece for widow and child."

"We would?" says Mr. Masterson.

"Your generosity overwhelms me, gentlemen!" Beanstone extends both hams for the C-notes as they are counted out. "I assure you, sirs, the Drovers Bank will do its part as well."

Hearts are touched. Murmurs of approbation linger over the marble.

"Now, sirs, if you'll just sign these receipts." Bill Beanstone bustles a space for them at a high table.

"Sign?" asks Mr. Masterson.

"A mere formality. For the Association—proof I've paid the reward so we'll be reimbursed. Here you are—here are pens, too."

Mr. Earp and Mr. Masterson look at each other, then belly up to the table, sign with a flourish, and turn over the receipts. Beanstone inspects one signature, guffaws, inspects the other, guffaws, and holds the sheets aloft.

"You'll never believe this, folks! Got a real sense of humor, these gents—but the joke's on us, I guess. This one's signed. 'W.B. Masterson!'"

Laughter.

"And this one 'W. Earp!'"

Laughter.

"Why in hell shell out for Harvey?" yells Bat over the four-cylinder frenzy of the Ford.

"Conscience!" Wyatt yells. "For that sheepshit shoot-out you pulled at the Knickerbocker Bar!"

"Five hundred's too much!"

"Be a big spender! We're on our way to sixty thousand!"

An hour later this is a different, debonair Wyatt, now that he has a large sum in long green in his poke. He sits at ease, foot cocked up on the dashboard while his chauffeur glues himself to the steering wheel. Spark and throttle levers are fully advanced, and the T tears along at 40 mph. There is considerable clanking in the rear seat compartment as two new shovels collide with the old Sharp's rifle. These they've purchased at a hardware store in Dodge on the theory that they can move wheat a hell of a lot faster with shovels and elbow grease than with bare hands. It's a hair after two o'clock. They intend to be all done and buttoned up and back in Dodge at the station with time to spare.

"What time's our trains?" Bat yells.

"Mine five-fifteen! Yours five-oh-five!"

Bat nods and dusts them along a gravel road due north of Garden of Eden. They are too smart to take the main highway to that metropolis—half of Dodge will be out looking for the abandoned loot, not to mention Jack Sughrue and his cohorts after the cash and the poor peace officer's remains. They keep therefore to the section roads, describing three sides of a rectangle in order to sneak into Garden of Eden from the east rather than the west. Bat has had no experience driving on gravel. The Tin Lizzie slips and slides like a trombone player on a pair of banana peels.

"Take it easy!" Wyatt yells. "I want to be rich before I'm dead!"

In rejoinder, Bat begins to sing "East Side, West Side" at the top of his voice.

They can see the trees, they can see the elevator glittering in the afternoon sun like a bar of pure gold. They turn south, and five minutes later reach the macadam highway and tool onto it on two wheels for the straight run, the last lap, and sure as the devil, once Bat has full speed up again, the red line on the Boyce Moto-Meter rises to "Danger—Steaming!" and a plume of steam gushes from the radiator.

"Slow down!" warns Wyatt.

"When I get home," bawls an oblivious Bat, "I'm gonna rent Rector's and put on a feed for Runyon and the gang they'll never forget!"

"Let 'er cool off!"

"Then I'm gonna put the Ginger Sisters in a suite at the Waldorf and strip 'em down and cover the bed with silver dollars and lay 'em both for Lady Liberty!"

They enter Garden of Eden and slew off the road to reach the rear of the elevator and coast to a stop and cut the engine and sit for a minute, staring, as the steam expires and the whistle dies. Then they get out of the car as though crippled. Then they walk to the tower like men who have been to Hell itself and come back alive though badly burned.

The dark green getaway Studebaker sits where they left it, one rear tire shredded. But in their absence a boxcar has been shunted along the railroad spur behind the elevator. It stands with doors open while a steady steam of wheat pours into it from the unload spout. By the doors stands L.D. Good and his jawbone and his miller's cap, one hand on the line which leads up to the cut-off in the spout. He sees them coming and jerks the line, cutting off the flow of grain.

"Back again, huh, boys?"

Cats have their tongues.

"You sure must need that nickel."

"What," says Bat, speaking with some difficulty, "what are you doing?"

"Loadin' wheat, that's what."

"Why," asks Wyatt, speaking with some difficulty, "why are you loading wheat?"

"Got a call for it, that's why."

Bat lays back his head and bays like a hound. "Why in hell'd you have to load it today!"

"Got the call for it today, that's why." L.D. jerks the line and the flow resumes. "Just after you left with them four deadies. Got a call for a carload and called the yard in Dodge and had 'em send a car and it come so I'm loadin' it. Two thousand bushels. About cleans us out."

"Where's it going?" asks Bat.

"Minneapolis," says the scaleman. "Into flour. Then back East into bread."

"Bread," Wyatt repeats.

"Best damn bread in the country. Made from the best damn wheat in the hull damn world. Kansas hard winter red."

They stand in silence with L.D. Good, transfixed by the fountain of wheat flowing from the spout into the boxcar. Now and then, unmistakably, there are weeds of green in the grain. They take out bandannas and give their noses long, lugubrious blows.

"Real enriched bread," proclaims a proud L.D. Good, scratching his jawbone. "Listen, boys, they'll serve this wheat to the tinhorns in the ritziest eateries in New York City!"

Later that afternoon, bags beside them, Mr. Earp and Mr. Masterson awaited their trains at the Santa Fe station. Upon return to Dodge, they had packed and split up, Bat to return the hired Ford, Wyatt to check them out of the O'Neal House.

"How much for the car?" Wyatt inquired.

"Not a cent. The gink said seeing's we're heroes, the ride was on him."

"Same thing at the hotel. Snotty kid at the desk said what we've done for Dodge, money couldn't buy."

They waited. Bat lit a Spud, Wyatt a Mexican Commerce. Bat inhaled. Wyatt drew. Bat leaned against the stone wall of the station for a spell, then moved around in a circle. Wyatt leaned against the station wall for a spell, then moved around. They looked across at the new Front Street. They looked up at the replica of Old Front Street, and beyond that, at Boot Hill.

"I know what you're thinking," said Bat. "But how in God's name could I know things'd turn out like this? Besides, you called the play."

Wyatt had no comment.

"Anyway," Bat philosophized, "half a loaf's better than none."

"Not funny," said Wyatt, spitting tobacco.

They leaned for a spell and moved around for a spell on the platform.

"What'll you do with your two grand?" asked Bat.

"Buy a good colt, I expect. Try to train it into a winner. What'll you do?"

"Oh, I dunno. Give Grogan a thou right off the bat—maybe that'll buy me some elbow room with Rothstein. The rest of it, I can probably run into a stake at pasteboards and the ponies."

"Sure you can."

Bat detected no irony. "Something on my mind, Wyatt. I told you I don't have any life insurance—never believed in it. The way I live, I could leave Emma poor as a church-mouse. I owe her more than that. Well, this has been some stunt. What I'd like to do, soon as I get home, is sit down and write this whole thing down. How we got together again in New York after all these years and came back to Dodge to rob the bank—the whole ball of wax. Then I'll stash it away in a strongbox and ask Em not to touch it till both of us are six feet under. Then she can sell it to some paper or library—should fetch her plenty. D'you have any objection?"

"Nope. Nobody'll believe it anyway."

"Well, they might, if I put it on paper myself—sucker born every minute. Make a hell of a story."

"You boys tourists?"

They swung around to meet the shifty eye of a very old coot who'd wheelchaired up behind them.

"Say, I recollect you!" said he. "Chinned with you the other day—ain't you the fellers kilt all them bank robbers?"

"Guilty," said Wyatt.

"My Gawd, that was some shootin'—my frien's Earp an' Masterson couldna done better!" enthused Methuselah. His nose was as red as before, his ten-gallon as battered, and from the smell of him he had his snootful.

"How're things going, old-timer?" asked Bat.

"Mighty slow. Not worth a pinch a dried owl dung. Say—you was the ones said when you left town we might do business. You leavin'?"

"Right quick."

"Well now listen." The gaffer shot a glance east and a glance west and chaired close to them and reached into his shirt front and fumbled out an old Colt. "I still got Masterson's pistola an' it's still for sale. Fifty bucks."

"Fifty!" objected Wyatt.

"Cheap. Dirt. Why, this is the gun Masterson gunned down Walker and Wagner with, after they murdered his brother Ed."

"The other day you said you'd take thirty."

"I did? I musta been dyin' a thirst. Well hell, awright. Thirty it is."

"What's your name, partner?" asked Wyatt.

"Vaughn. Orlie Vaughn."

"Tell you what, Orlie. You hang on to the gun. But here." Wyatt peeled a packet out of an inside pocket and peeled off a ten and a twenty. "Here's your thirty—and good luck to you."

"That's mighty white a you," wheezed Orlie Vaughn, stuffing the bills into a shirt pocket. "Guess the country ain't goin' t'hell after all."

225

"And here." Bat pulled from his armpit another Peacemaker and laid it in the plainsman's lap. "There's a real souvenir to sell."

"Say, what is this—Chris'mas?" Orlie acknowledged the gift with a toss of his head. "I'm just obliged all t'pieces."

"You can cut some notches and tell the tourists that persuader belonged to your friend Bat Masterson himself," added Bat.

"Allus do." The old toper gave them a gap-tooth grin. "I tell 'em all that. Them dudes don't know shit from apple butter. Thank you, boys—nice t'meet some Christians for a change."

Orlie Vaughn doffed his ten-gallon, wheeled to the station wall, parked his chair, hopped out of it, and money in one hand, new merchandise in the other, overcame his hip handicap sufficiently to spry across Front Street and into the Long Branch Pharmacy to fill a prescription.

Just as that door closed, the door of the Popular Cafe opened, and across the street to the Santa Fe station tripped two strapping girlies in waitress uniforms with ticking aprons—Miss Birdie and Miss Dyjean Fedder. This shameless sortie across Front Street in broad daylight to consort with two gentlemen from out of town might make them the talk of it, but decorum, their bright eyes declared, and their flushed cheeks, be damned. Each carried something in a paper sack.

"Hullo, Cupcake," said Bat to Birdie.

"Evening, ma'am," said Wyatt to Dyjean.

"Oooooh, what you did!" gasped Birdie.

"We saw the bodies!" gasped Dyjean.

"A bagatelle," said Bat, flipping his Spud.

"Just doing our duty," said Wyatt, heeling his Mexican Commerce.

"We heard you claimed you're Wells-Fargo agents," said Birdie. "What a laugh!"

"Had to say something," said Bat.

"We're the only ones in town really know," said Dyjean. "Think of that!"

"Don't," Wyatt admonished. "Just forget us."

"We'll never!" cried Birdie.

"Never, ever!" cried Dyjean.

"D'you really have to leave?" begged Birdie.

"Can't you stay over tonight?" begged Dyjean.

"Gotta give my regards to Broadway," said Bat.

" 'Parting is such sweet sorrow,' " said Wyatt.

"If you'll give us your address," said Birdie, "we'll write to you."

"I move around a lot," said Bat.

"Yes I guess not," said Wyatt.

"Will you ever come back?" asked Dyjean.

"We've never left," said Wyatt.

"There'll always be a little bit of Masterson and Earp in Dodge," said Bat brightly.

"Well listen, then," said Birdie. She and Dyjean looked north and looked south and came close to the two men and readied paper sacks. "We brought something for you to autograph. Got a pen?"

"Right here," said Bat, pulling his Parker.

"Then will you autograph these for us?"

Birdie and Dyjean brought forth from the sacks, as surreptitiously as possible, two massive cotton brassieres.

"Ahem," said Bat. "Of course."

"Proud to," said Wyatt.

Bat signed his name across a capacious cup, then handed

pen to Wyatt, who signed Dyjean's.

"Hey, wait a minute," said Birdie, thinking fast. "You both better autograph both."

"Oh, Birdie!" said Dyjean.

"You're right," said Wyatt, who signed Birdie's and proffered the Parker to Bat, who signed Dyjean's.

The Fedder cousins stuffed brassieres into the sacks clumsily due to the dew in their eyes.

"Goodbye, Bat," sighed Birdie, and kissed him on the cheek, then remembered to kiss Wyatt.

"Goodbye, Wyatt," said Dyjean, and kissed him on the cheek, then remembered to kiss Bat.

"Goodbye, my dears," said Bat.

"A pleasure meeting you," said Wyatt.

"We won't tell," promised Birdie.

"Not till we're old ladies," promised Dyjean.

"You two'll never be old," said the gallant Wyatt.

"Neither will you!" they cried, and rushed back across the street with sacks clasped to their bountiful bosoms.

They leaned against the station wall a spell and moved around a spell. Bat's train east was supposed to show in five minutes.

"Amoor, amoor," reflected Mr. Masterson.

"They can talk about a bird in the hand till they're blue in the face," reflected Mr. Earp. "I'll take two in the bush anytime."

Around the corner of the station hustled a husky young gent wearing a polka-dot necktie and a smile of relief and offering a glad hand.

228

"Mr. Earp? Mr. Masterson? Sure glad I caught up with you in time."

"Oh?" said Mr. Earp.

"Oh?" said Mr. Masterson.

"I'm Larry Deger, Mayor of Dodge, and I've got a job to do before you get away."

"Oh?"

"Oh?"

"Yessiree. The Town Council just had a meeting over at the Long Branch Pharmacy."

"Blue or orange?" Mr. Masterson inquired.

Mr. Deger colored. "We passed a resolution— don't know who you are, but after what you did for Dodge today—putting us on the map again—it don't matter. We want you to have these."

He held up two shiny, six-pointed badges with the inscription "Marshal Dodge City." "As mayor," said His Honor, "I now declare you Honorary Marshals of Dodge City, with all rights and privileges thereto pertaining."

"Why, thank you!" said Mr. Masterson.

"Much obliged," said Mr. Earp.

Mayor Deger pinned badges on lapels and once again offered his hand, which was accepted this time with smiles of civic virtue.

"Thank you, gents. I've got to get along now, but you ever come back to Dodge, we'll sure roll out the red carpet. Oh, say—we found the crooks' guns in the back of your car. Three automatics and what they call—I think they call it a submachine gun. Oh, and an old buffalo gun—how they got that I'll never know. Anyway, sheriff's got 'em all now, but they're rightfully yours. He's still out looking for the loot. I can bring 'em if you want 'em."

"Do we!" said Mr. Masterson.

229

"No," said Mr. Earp.

"No?" blurted Mr. Masterson.

"No," said Mr. Earp. "Dodge has treated us first class, and we'd like to repay the favor. Artillery like that'll boost the tourist trade. Why don't you put 'em under glass in the Beeson Museum?"

"What in hell did you say no for?" demanded Bat as soon as Larry Deger had decamped around the corner. "You know what that tommy gun's worth in my neck of the woods? That piece might've got me off the hook with Rothstein!"

Wyatt would have responded, but just then they heard it—Bat's choo-choo, the Santa Fe "Pioneer," clanging into Dodge eastbound for Chicago. They looked at each other. The time had come.

"Well," said Bat.

"Well," said Wyatt.

The train hissed in, brakes squealing, couplings clunking. This was one Harvey Wadsworth wouldn't meet. Bat picked up his bag.

"Take care of yourself," said Bat. "A man your age—"

"My age?"

"Okeh, our age."

"My best to Emma."

"My best to Josie."

"You write, I will."

"I will."

They walked together down the train.

"Listen," said Bat. "Anytime you get a craving for the big city again, the bright lights and all, you let me know."

"Not likely."

They stopped at the car steps and shook hands.

"So long, Wyatt."

"Take care of yourself, Bat."

"Just one thing I wanna know, pal," said Bat. "Did you have a good time?"

"I did," said sobersides Wyatt. "Maybe the best damn time I ever had in my life."

Then, suddenly, they grinned at each other like kids and shook hands again, hard, and William Barclay Masterson tipped his derby to the town and the past and went up the steps fast because they didn't trust their tear ducts because, the truth was, neither of them expected to see the other again in Dodge or New York City or, for that matter, this world.

He has ten minutes more to wait. He leans against the station wall and moves around and then sits down in Orlie Vaughn's wheelchair. His gimp knee aches and the crick in his shoulder and he is dead tired and a hundred years old and lonesome as hell and Los Angeles is a million miles away and sometimes, like now, there have been too many times on a trigger and too many wets of the whistle and too many pulchritudinous tits and too many good men gone including brothers—even for him. He tries to see Front Street clearly and can't, so takes out a bandanna and wipes his eyes. Then he can, and who should cross the street, coming at him on ladder legs, but the snotnose star reporter for the Dodge City *Daily Globe*. Wyatt stands up, annoyed at himself for being caught in a wheelchair, and pretends to be shining his honorary marshal's badge with a coatsleeve. He is glad, actually, to see the stringbean again. He told Bat he's had a damn good time, and meant it, and now the fun isn't over. He's about to have some more.

"There you are!" says Dudley Robison, balancing his straw boater.

"Mr. Robison."

"Where's your friend?"

"Just pulled out, eastbound."

"I'm sorry to hear that—I had a bone to pick with him. And I wanted to question you both."

"Half a loaf's better than none."

"I guess so." Dudley is obviously bitter. "But he told me tomorrow morning at six o'clock."

"Company keeps us hopping," says Wyatt.

"Unh-huh." The newshawk whips out pad and pencil and puts on a reportorial face. "That's the first thing. For your information, sir, I took the trouble to wire Wells-Fargo in San Francisco. I asked them if they have two agents working here in Dodge and I just got the answer. No, they don't. They do not."

"Confidential," smiles Wyatt.

"Unh-huh." Dudley is rapidly working up a dander. "Sir, if you don't mind my saying so, there's something fishy about all this. The sheriff still hasn't found the bank money, and neither's anybody else. I intend to get to the bottom of things."

"Good for you."

Dudley has a long nose. He gives it a petulant pull. "Now I expect you to answer my questions, old-timer. First off, I want to hear in your own words exactly what happened over at Garden of Eden this morning."

"Come here, Dudley."

"What?"

232

"Come close."

Dudley hesitates. Wyatt yanks him by both arms so close that they could rub noses.

"Now take your hand and put it inside my coat, up by the left shoulder. See what you feel."

Slats does. And when he touches the steel, when his fingers shape the butt of the big .45, his face turns pale yellow, as though he's coming down with some fearful, fatal malady.

"Now listen, Sonny," says Wyatt into the other's nostrils. He freezes his eyes and grims up like a storm. "One of two things. Either you remove your proboscis from my business and get your skinny, snoopy, sorrowful ass out of here—or."

"Or?" whispers the youngster.

"Or I'll take what you're touching and bat you over the head with it the way Wyatt Earp used to do and two weeks from now you'll still be on ice."

Dudley Robison withdraws his hand very slowly and backs off and turns around and moves very slowly across Front Street as though he's just been vouchsafed the deepest, darkest secrets of sex.

After that he feels full of beans again. The sun is shining low in the blue sky and it's a late and loamy afternoon in May and he can hear his train now, the "Trooper," clanging into Dodge westbound for the City of Angels. He rigs his hat and tie. The "Trooper" hisses in, brakes squealing, couplings clunking, and as he is about to pick up his valise he is accosted by a butcher boy. The kid is twelve or so, freckled and bright as a dollar, with hair which needs a comb and cheeks a scrub and stockings a hoist up to his knickers. Hung by a cord around his neck is a wooden tray on which is arrayed his meager stock in trade.

"Last chance to buy, Mister. Chewing gum, candy bars, apples, cigars—you name it, I got it."

"How about a Mexican Commerce?"

"Nope. They're too stinky. How 'bout a Havana Grand—two for a quarter?"

"A quarter? That's too dear." Wyatt rearranges some splayed hairs in his mustache. "A butcher boy, huh? What do you calculate to do when you get some long in your legs?"

"Gonna be a peace officer—ride a motorcycle and catch crooks. Baroom! Baroom! Bang! Bang!"

"Um. You could get shot, too."

"Aw, not me."

Wyatt nods. "Tell you what—you skin across the street and bring me back a couple Mexican Commerce. I'll watch your tray. Give you a dime for the smokes and a nickel for the trip."

"Let's see the money, Mister."

"Let's see the cigars, Buster."

Boy and man appraise each other. The man evidently passes muster, for after a moment the boy bangs his tray down by the station wall and scoots off across Front Street like a scared rabbit. The man watches him, thinks about him, then stoops, selects two Havana Grands, puts them away in a pocket, reaches under his coat, pulls out an old Colt, and lays it on the tray among the apples. He picks up his bag and strides down the platform past several cars and stops at some steps. Wyatt Berry Stapp Earp has one last look at Dodge, inflates his chest to get full benefit of his marshal's badge, then climbs aboard humming a tune he's picked up from Bat, a snappy ditty called "Yacka Hula Hickey Dula."

Author's Note

There it was, Bat's tall and thrilling tale, in his own authenticated hand—but what the devil was I to do with it? I was in a barrel with my own badger, and I did not know which of us would get out alive.

As I have said, I locked away the four pages in 1970 and busied myself writing novels. In my spare time, however, I pondered the miracle of the movement of the Masterson MS. from Bat's pen to my own safe-deposit box—a journey covering fifty-four years—and eventually explained it to my satisfaction. Before parting with Winchell that afternoon in Scottsdale (I never saw him again), I chanced to ask if Damon Runyon had told him anything more about the transaction between himself and Emma Masterson. He had. According to the lady, Runyon said, Bat wrote out the four pages with his Parker in their living room in the early morning hours of May 7 in 1916 on his return to New York (from whence his wife did not learn till later), woke her, and confessed he was sorry he had never had his life insured. But now, he said, to compensate, he was stashing this thing he'd just written in a strongbox at their branch of the Bowery Bank, and giving her the key. She was not, absolutely not, to open the box and read it until after his death and that of his old sidekick Wyatt Earp, which she would see in the papers when Wyatt went because much would be made of him. She was then to take the pages to a newspaper or a library and offer them for sale. They would, if he was any judge, fetch her a goodly sum, as much as any insurance policy he could have afforded. All this, Winchell said, had required Runyon half an hour and several cups of coffee to scribble laboriously on a copy pad that night in 1945 in the Stork Club.

(It tallied. I had seen with my own eyes, in the Masterson Collection in Topeka, a letter from Emma Masterson to her niece sent shortly after Bat's death in which she mentioned, besides the fact that "his feet were so cold... he wore wollin [sic] stockings in bed at nights," that "Your Uncle Bat never believed in life insurance.")

For a writer of fiction, the rest was easy to reconstruct. Five years later, the old gambler cashed in his chips. For seven more, his widow waited. She may have needed money, but she was a woman of spunk, a suffragette, she'd been faithful to her marriage vows and still loved a man who, she was sure, had been a model of fidelity. So she waited, bless her, and watched the papers. And when, on January 13, 1929, the passing of Wyatt Earp made front pages, she made a beeline for the Bowery Bank, opened the box—and like Pandora wished to hell she hadn't. The Ginger Sisters? Birdie and Dyjean Fedder? Bat Masterson a would-have-been bank robber? Wyatt Earp his willing accomplice? Lord have mercy! Poor she might be, but she'd sell her body to the highest bidder before she'd hang such scandalous linen in Times Square!

Poor she was, indeed, and each year her widow's mite became a mite less. By 1931 she was desperate. Swallowing her pride, she went to Damon Runyon with the four shameful pages. He read them, was as shocked as she, and unwilling to have his friend and a towering folklore figure take a tumble should they be made public, offered

236

her a thousand dollars for them plus his word that they would never see a typesetter. She accepted with relief. Emma Masterson died at seventy-five, on July 12, 1932, in a small room at the Hotel Stratford, certain, I expect, that her spouse would approve what she had done.

Perhaps he did, perhaps he didn't. And whether or not he approved Runyon's bequest of his manuscript to Walter Winchell in 1945, and the latter's gift of it to me in 1970, there is no point in speculating. With the death of Winchell in 1972 I became the last man in the line—and I was trustee now not only of Mr. Masterson's reputation but that of Mr. Earp as well.

I was whipsawed. To a writer, I have earlier remarked, ink is more potent than strong drink, print a prospect more interesting than sex. But I had given my word, and every time I was tempted to break it, Winchell's irascible shade put a finger to its lips. Yet every time I steeled myself, Bat's ghost, and Wyatt's, hoglegs in hands, poked me in the ribs with them, and dusty voices in my ear urged, "Shoot the works, Swarthout! Have some fun!"

In the end they won. I succumbed. And just as coincidence had concealed their intended robbery of the Drovers Bank of Dodge City, so that they came out of it smelling like roses, luck let me perceive in time a way to wriggle out from between rock and my hard place. I could publish their story after all. I could publish it not as fact but as fiction. I could write a novel based on it, a kind of "Eastern Western," and in so doing have the fun they urged me to have. And I had other, unselfish, excuses. If, in their heyday, Bat and Wyatt had looked upon the wine when it was red, a book about them set in 1916 would demonstrate that even in decline they could still cut the mustard as marvelously as men half their age. It would constitute their terminal hoot at eternity. And they might sleep the better for such a book, these dear old Colts. Confession in hardcover would get a last incredible caper off their chests.

I cleared my desk. In 1981, after eleven years of slugging it out with guilt and ego, I sidestepped ethics and got to work. (Many kind souls assisted, although I kept the subject close to my vest. Carolyn Lake, for example, daughter of Stuart N. Lake, Earp's official biographer, granted gracious permission to reproduce the tintype I have placed on the back jacket. It was made in 1876, when Bat, standing, was twenty-three and Wyatt twenty-eight and both were deputy sheriffs of Ford County.) I stuck like Luke McGlue to the skeleton of their adventure as Bat had set it down, using his names and dates but shifting scene and embellishing incident to put my own brand on the story— the rustler's wont, the novelist's prerogative. I finished *The Old Colts* last year, having ballooned Bat's few hundred words into seventy-five lovely thousand, and sent it off to my publishers.

There was a gasp. They were as dubious as I had been in the beginning. They asked to see the four-page MS. and whatever supporting correspondence I had. These I provided, and after long silence my editor informed me that based on their own authentication, by manuscript people at the Morgan Library and the New York Historical Society, it was their decision to publish. They loved the book, he apologized, but surely I could understand their dumbfoundment on first reading, their incredulity on second. I could.

I sat back then and awaited the book with an alloy of anticipation and apprehension. Critics and historians would charge me at the least, I was warned, with trying to whittle Earp and Masterson down to my own insignificant size. I would be called in print a liar, an asshole, a sensationalist, a traducer of character, a slinger of mud at sacred American myths. Should the assaults become too vicious, however, I had a derringer up my sleeve. I had what Bat Masterson himself had written, in brownish ink on yellow paper, with authority to back my play, and should push come to shove, I would draw and fire.

I had it then. God's blood, I do not now. Some months prior to the appearance of *The Old Colts* there occurred a tragic concatenation of events, as tragic as the call for a boxcar of wheat to be unloaded from the elevator in Garden of Eden before the eyes of our hapless heroes. I had the four holograph pages spread out on my desk one day. It was a balmy morning in Scottsdale, the windows were open, and I was unexpectedly called away from the house. Since my wife was also absent, the premises were shared by our cleaning woman and a stray, wild cat we had recently adopted and christened "Bat." I can only surmise that a ruffian breeze wafted the pages to the floor; that the cat, which we were trying to paper-train because it turned up its nose at the litter box, used the pages for its natural purposes; that the cleaning woman disposed of them in the garbage can out front; that the garbage men came by on their appointed rounds; and—the reader knows the rest, and may imagine the magnitude of my loss, not to mention the loss to the literature of the West.

Some will sneer, I suppose, that this served me right. Others will whisper that it was neither fate nor a feline, but Bat and Wyatt, jealous of their legend, reaching out of the mists to larrup me over the head with gunbarrels, lug me away, see me tried for slander and sentenced to life in a calaboose of shame and futility. In any case, I am inconsolable. What a calamitous, cat-shit conclusion!

Wyatt Earp, 1928

*"The greatest consolation I have
in growing old is the hope that
after I'm gone they'll grant me
the peaceful obscurity I haven't
been able to get in life."*

**William Jerome's poetic farewell to
his friend in the** Morning Telegraph

*Goodbye, Bat.
They never heard you blat
About the things you did out West—
You wasn't built like that.*

*That great big golden heart of yours,
It wouldn't harm a cat.
Sweet as a "gal," so long old pal,
Goodbye, Bat.*